The Terror

THE TERROR

Western Stories

B. M. Bower

edited by
Kate Baird Anderson

Five Star • Waterville, Maine

First Edition
First Printing: February 2003

Published in 2003 in conjunction with
Golden West Literary Agency.

Set in 11 pt. Plantin.

Printed in the United States on permanent paper.

Library of Congress Cataloging-in-Publication Data

Bower, B. M., 1874–1940.
    The terror : western stories / by B. M. Bower ; edited by
Kate Baird Anderson.
        p. cm.
    Contents: Finders is keepers—From hell to Kilpatrick's
—The sheepherder—The vanguard of the Philistines—The
deserter—The terror—The problem—A throne for a day
—The white thread—The western tone—Hawkins—The
infernal feminine.
    ISBN 0-7862-3775-9 (hc : alk. paper)
    1. Western stories. I. Anderson, Kate Baird. II. Title.
PS3503.O8193 T47 2003
    813'.52—dc21   2002033885

The Terror

Table of Contents

Foreword

Around a hundred and fifty short stories, many magazine novelettes and serials, and sixty-five hard cover books by B. M. Bower appeared in print during her long career. She was the first woman in the 20th Century to make a living writing Western fiction and, in my opinion, was the most creative.

Bower used standard pulp formulas for stories that presented "the clear article" as honestly as possible, but with unique twists. Her trademark wry humor blended well with Westerners' customary reverse sarcasm. Her realistic characters were ordinary humans struggling with the usual desires, weaknesses, and virtues in difficult circumstances and hazardous environments. Women often played major rôles. Contrary to editors' preferences for nostalgia, she included innovations like trains, telephones, automobiles, airplanes, electrical appliances, wireless radio, and motion pictures—and often referred to classic and contemporary music, literature, psychology, science, medicine, and religion. Bower and her work truly kept up with the times.

Her best-known stories were about the Flying U outfit in North Central Montana. CHIP OF THE FLYING U, her first book, came out in 1906 with Western artist and friend Charles M. Russell's illustrations. In time, the book's popularity rivaled Owen Wister's 1902 blockbuster, THE VIRGINIAN, an instant best seller, now considered the first 20th Century Western classic. CHIP, in a similar down-to-earth style enhanced by ironic humor, is the second classic.

Wister was a well-born, college-educated Easterner with a

rosy, romantic view of the West before he visited Wyoming. Aristocratic cattle barons welcomed him as a published author and man of quality. The eloquent language and clean style of THE VIRGINIAN, along with the author's impeccable credentials, generated glowing reviews from Eastern critics. They declared the book a must have for respectable public and family libraries, a first for Western fiction.

Bertha Muzzy began at the bottom of the social and educational scale, the youngest daughter of hard-working, populist-minded farmers, her only assets a decent Northern Baptist upbringing on various Minnesota farms, unusual intelligence, inborn talent with words, unquenchable curiosity, and a writer's eye and ear. Her formal education had ended in Otter Tail County in 1883 with the rural equivalent of the eighth grade, but her father encouraged her voracious reading habit as a possible remedy. The strategy succeeded. Her work compares quite favorably with Wister's and that of other well-educated contemporaries.

The Muzzys moved to a prairie farm near Great Falls, Montana in 1889; Bertha turned eighteen that year. She had supported herself from the age of fourteen teaching in Minnesota's rural schools, and that first Montana winter agreed to one more term in an isolated ranching community fifty miles south of Great Falls. Although she was just five feet tall, her natural poise and air of authority had helped her deal with older and bigger students—one look usually subdued the most recalcitrant. Properly upswept bronze-auburn hair, large, expressive hazel eyes, a stubborn chin, and a fashionably generous figure also helped "teacher" appear more mature. She returned home ill the following March and swore off teaching forever.

In 1890 she married a young neighbor, Clayton Joseph Bower, and settled in Great Falls. The Bowers moved to Big

Sandy in 1897. The primitive stock shipping point on the Montana Central branch of The Great Northern Railway anchored a vast area of arid open range. The hamlet offered sprawling stockyards, a general store, clapboard schoolhouse, three saloons, two hotels, and not much else to roughly a hundred permanent residents—including local whores—and area ranchers. It had no church, doctor, or newspaper, and only one crippled deputy sheriff. Indians from two reservations and a group of homeless wanderers worked and traded there. Mrs. Bower was one of the few respectable white women in the sparsely populated country. As a safely married lady, she became a popular partner at area dances and socials. She also listened attentively to people's stories, and retained much of what she heard.

In that last remnant of the most remote but rapidly changing Wild West, one important element remained active. For decades outlaws like Butch Cassidy and Kid Curry had found refuge and friends in and around the Bear Paw Mountains, Little Rockies, and Missouri River breaks, and continued their visits. Rustlers, Indians, and whisky smugglers still used the old outlaw trails running across the Canadian border. Ranchers who valued their health asked no personal questions of newcomers. As long as a man behaved and did his work, hosts and bosses ignored misdeeds committed elsewhere.

None of this affected the Bower family directly, but it strengthened Bertha's resolve to become independent. Writing for pulp magazines seemed the best way to earn money at home without capital or special training, but her first efforts brought no sales. William "Bill" Sinclair, a Canadian cowpuncher known locally as Fiddleback, boarded with the family over a couple of winters, and suggested Mrs. Bower might do better writing about the real thing, instead of

11

producing unsuccessful "little romances". The self-educated, semi-Socialist top hand and fellow maverick—nine years younger than his hostess—also wanted a writing career. The two soon found other mutual interests.

Then Albert L. Sessions, editor of Street & Smith's classy *Ainslee's, the Magazine that Entertains*, bought some of Bertha M. Bower's new stories. He liked the authentic but clean dialogue that retained the general effect of the vulgar, profane language men used among themselves—and censored around women, especially Mrs. Bower—without quoting it directly. He asked for a longer novelette in the same style and setting. The result was "Chip, of the Flying U", with Bill Sinclair as Bertha's consultant for "range stuff". It became the lead story in the October, 1904 issue of *The Popular Magazine*, a nearly moribund Street & Smith publication newly revamped and edited by Charles MacLean. The biggest publisher of pulps in the country had helped O. Henry, Upton Sinclair, Theodore Dreiser, and other up-and-coming authors start professional careers. Bertha received the same hand up when MacLean became her mentor and friend—by mail. She signed her first writing contract with Street & Smith Publications in 1905, got a divorce, and married Bertrand W. Sinclair, Bill's new pen name.

Astute Charles MacLean had discovered his protégée was a matronly-looking wife and mother. Revealing that would likely kill sales and ruin her new career as well as her social reputation. She was to use the pen name B. M. Bower exclusively, and keep her feminine identity a secret. Thus few fans ever learned the author was not a range-bred man until they saw the newspaper obituary in July, 1940—and some rejected outright the accompanying photo of a smiling woman in a soft Stetson hat.

B. M. Bower got a second professional boost in 1912 when Little, Brown agreed to issue LONESOME LAND, her first serious, semi-autobiographical novel, in 1912. It was a grand literary success. From then on, as she wandered through the West, she wrote two novels a year for Little, Brown—always as B. M. Bower. Many silent Western films, with stars like Tom Mix and Hoot Gibson, were based on Bower stories. Her third marriage in 1920 led to a challenging mining venture in Nevada and several successful novels set in the Southwest desert. During the Depression of the 1930s, when income dropped drastically, she found affordable refuge on the Oregon coast, and kept on writing.

Like others of her generation, my unusual grandmother's complex, productive life bridged the cataclysmic changes of the late 19th Century and the early 20th Century. She started an autobiography several times, but never completed it; back trails held little interest for her. Fortunately my mother protected the surviving papers. They provided new insights and a firm foundation for the definitive biography I now have under way with Bower's original title, BREAK YOUR OWN TRAIL.

Short stories were the foundation of B. M. Bower's long career, as they were for most popular fiction authors in her time. The language of almost a century ago is still clear, and themes remain timely. I have restored texts in this collection from original manuscripts where possible. I have *not* changed or deleted any material deemed unacceptable by some contemporary standards. That would be totalitarian censorship of the most grievous kind. Proponents of currently fashionable political correctness should set aside their prejudices and scalpels if they want to enjoy these tales as Bower's fans did.

B. M. Bower's stories were valuable records of Western

history and people just as she experienced and interpreted them. She would be so pleased that her literary snapshots are still interesting and entertaining in the 21st Century.

Kate Baird Anderson
Bentonville, Arkansas

Finders Is Keepers

During the Depression of the 1930s, Bower's income from magazine serial rights dropped sharply, so she returned to short stories. "Finders Is Keepers" appeared in the July, 1933 issue of *West*. The story is set in 1887 when the Montana Central Railroad first came to Big Sandy, the model for Dry Lake. Flying U foreman, Chip Bennett, the "finder", happens upon a rare and moving cow funeral for a butchered calf. In a burst of compassion, Chip hires the starving, handicapped slayer. As usual, the Flying U boys unmercifully haze the huge, oddly meek newcomer they label Dickybird, unaware that his iron control is all that stands between them and death. A similar tragic figure appeared as a main character in THE HAUNTED HILLS (Little, Brown, 1934), one of Bower's finest Western mysteries.

On a hot day in summer, a brockle-faced old range cow waded out of a muddy pool and started up across the narrow flat to where her calf was sleeping through the hot hours in the shade of a chokecherry thicket. The lazy wind was behind her. She loitered along, nipping choice tufts of grass as she went. Once she stopped and twisted herself into grotesque contortion, licking a spot high on her flank where a tick had fastened himself last spring and left behind him a permanent itch. When she unwound herself afterward and looked like a cow again, she uttered a languid *moo* to let her calf know she was coming, and walked on. There was no sound or stir from the chokecherry shade. The cow *mooed* again and walked a little faster.

The tricky breeze swirled in from the north past the thicket. The cow's head went up and she stood in her tracks, sniffing and staring. Then with a weird and terrible bellow she started forward at an awkward gallop. In the cool shade of the thicket she tore at the grass and sent clods over her back, kneeling and goring blue harebells and Indian paintbrush with her horns between her frantic pawing. And all the while that eerie blood call went rumbling up to shrill crescendo, dying away to throaty gasps and mutterings.

Down by Flying U Creek, a big red steer surged to his feet in the trampled dust of the willows, bawled answer to the call, and started for the cherry thicket at a trot, bellowing that strange, unforgettable blood call of the cattle as he went. From all directions, the herd came bawling to join the cow and the steer, where they pawed and gored the earth and bellowed with their tongues straining sidewise down over their jaws like tired dogs. Soon there were fifty performers at the strange ceremonial, and more were coming on the run.

Then came Chip Bennett with his big gray hat tilted to shade his face from the sun. Stirrups thrust forward, lean young body slanted back, he rode down the steep high bluff from the north, curious to see what all the commotion was about. And presently with shrill yells that the cattle knew and heeded, helped by his swinging rope end that whacked the more persistent mourners, he arrived at the center of the gathering and stopped beside the thing that had caused all the uproar.

A spotted calf lay there with its throat slit and one hindquarter skinned out of its hide. Vandalism. Thievery and insolent waste, with no attempt to hide the evidence of the wanton crime. The kill was so fresh that Chip eyed the thicket sharply as he yanked his carbine from its saddle scabbard and pulled off his gloves, tucking them swiftly under his belt. Whoever killed that calf was close by, he knew that much— and, if they thought they were going to get away with it, they had another think coming, that was all.

Just then the breeze blew again down off the bench to the north, and with it came a whiff of wood smoke from the grassy draw behind the thicket. He reined his horse that way, keeping him on the grass. With the continued bedlam of the excited cattle there was not much danger of being heard, so he walked his horse within ten feet of the fire before he was discovered.

A great hulk of a man squatted on his heels watching a thick slice of veal steak threaded on the prongs of a forked cherry stick, sizzling over the fire. The flame and smoke licked at the meat—he had not waited for coals. A thick mop of black hair straggled down over his heavy brows. Jaws and chin were blanketed beneath a ten-day beard as black as his hair. His mouth was curtained behind a heavy black mustache. Beady black eyes watched the meat as a hungry dog would watch.

"Well, help yourself," Chip invited with angry sarcasm, after a minute or two of silent observation.

"I'm goin' to," the man said in a curiously diffident tone. "I ain't et fer two days."

"There's plenty of game in the country," Chip said sternly. "You didn't have to butcher a calf, did yuh?"

The fellow nodded, wolfing the half-cooked meat in a way Chip was ashamed to watch. "I . . . ain't got no gun," he mumbled apologetically while he chewed. "I couldn't git no game. Had to wait till I could sink m' loop on a calf."

Chip turned away from that famished feeding. Abruptly he twisted himself in the saddle and untied a package from behind the cantle. He unwrapped two thick sandwiches, took up one, and faced forward. "Here," he said gruffly. "Throw this into yuh." He tossed it as he would toss a bone to a hungry dog.

Like a hungry dog the man caught it, stuffed his mouth with pot roasted meat and sourdough bread.

Chip looked away again, taking in the makeshift camp. A horse stood back in the shade where a small spring seeped out of the hillside. A gaunt dispirited animal, standing with sagging lip, one fore hoof held so that it barely touched the ground. With one glance, Chip read the signs and faced forward again.

"Horse lame?"

"Uhn-huh. Stepped in a badger hole and sprained his shoulder, right out here on the flat. I been waitin' for 'im to git over it."

"What you doing for it? Got any liniment?"

"Uhn-uh. Been usin' cold water on it."

Chip got out his smoking material and built himself a cigarette, meticulously tearing a tiny strip off the paper before he troughed it for the tobacco, as was his habit.

"Can he walk at all?"

"Gits around on three legs. I can't ride 'im a-tall."

"Hell, you've got two feet, haven't yuh?" Chip drew a match sharply along the wild-rose border of his saddle. "You're only about four miles from camp. You could have walked in and got grub."

The man looked up from skewering a fresh slice of meat on the forked stick. "I don't know this country. Didn't know there was a ranch within twenty mile uh here. I couldn't walk that fur . . . my feet's no good fer walkin'. Too little fer m' body."

Chip saw that he spoke the truth. He had the smallest feet Chip had ever seen on a man. His boots looked about the right size for a woman, too small for some Chip knew.

"I figured on ridin' to the Flyin' U and tryin' to git a job," the man was saying humbly. "I'd like to work out the price of this calf, anyway. I ain't no cow thief, but when a feller's starvin', he don't stop fer no brand. I found that out."

"Well, you can tell that to the boss. I expect he'll let you square yourself somehow. I dunno . . . that's for him to say." Chip lifted the reins. "Better throw the saddle on your horse and start leading him up the creek. You can take it slow as you like, but keep going. I'll probably overtake you before you hit camp." He bit his lip, then asked a touchy question. "What name do you go by?"

"My own," the man told him with his first flash of spirit. "Dick Bird."

"Well, eat this other sandwich if you want it. I don't. You're liable to get a bellyache if you gorge yourself on that veal. I'll see yuh later, Bird. Maybe I can put in a word for yuh with the old man if you're on the level."

"I . . . I won't fergit it," Dick Bird stammered, catching the sandwich in both hands. "I sure don't know how I can thank yuh. . . ."

"Well, don't try." Chip wheeled his horse in its tracks and rode away, trying not to feel too sorry for the poor devil. Wondering, too, whether he had not been too soft and easy with the fellow. Maybe he had lied about not having any gun to shoot game. Maybe he was on the dodge and was afraid to shoot and run the risk of having someone hear the shot. Dick Bird might not be his name at all. He also thought he had been a fool not to go and look that horse over for himself. No use now, though. But if the fellow didn't mosey along up the creek like he was told, Chip meant to land on him like a wolf for that calf butchering.

But there was no need to concern himself over his credulity. Two hours later, having cut short his ride because of his worry, Chip rode back into the draw to find it deserted and the fire carefully doused with water. Three miles up the creek, Dick Bird was tilting along on his number-four boots, his black horse, painfully hobbling on three legs, behind him. Chip was so relieved that he stopped and persuaded Bird to leave the horse there for the present; and he pulled a foot from one stirrup and offered the man a lift to camp.

That evening, the Happy Family eyed the newcomer appraisingly when they assembled for supper and heard that he was going to work. With sidelong glances they gauged the enormous strength of his shoulders, the set of his ugly bullet head on his thick neck. Even when he had shaved off his beard, he looked mean and dangerous. The length of his arms and the size of his hands were amazing, and, when he walked on his little feet, he looked topheavy and about as safe as a gorilla.

It took them a full month to realize that Dick Bird would not hurt a fly. That was about the time they began calling him Dickybird to his face, and to josh Chip openly about the reasons why his Bird wouldn't sing. They advised cuttle-bone and hemp (seeds-ed). They also surmised that he must be molting.

Then they drifted into the habit of doing and saying things to get a chirp out of the giant Dickybird. They couldn't. They teased him, they framed him, they made him the butt of all the camp jokes and horseplay. Chip headed them off whenever he could, and took their jibes, giving back as good as he got. But he couldn't save the Dickybird altogether, and he used to get him off somewhere every few days, and implore him to go in and clean up on the bunch.

"They'll let yuh alone, once you bloody a nose or two," he

would argue impatiently. "Hell, you could lick even Shorty, if you went right after him, Bird. Next time they start throwing it into you, why don't you haul off and paste whoever comes handy?"

"I . . . I don't s'pose they mean nothin'," Dick Bird would stammer, not meeting Chip's eyes. "I wouldn't want to have no trouble with 'em. All I want is to git along nice and peaceable with everybody."

"Oh, all right. Have it your way," Chip growled the last time he labored with Bird. "I don't suppose there's any law against lying down and letting them walk on you, if you like it." He looked at the man wonderingly. "I sure don't savvy you, that's all."

"I . . . I don't guess I savvy myself any too well, either," Bird confessed. "I just . . . don't want any fuss."

"No-o," Chip said dryly, "I guess you don't." But it did grind him to see a man with all that muscle take the insults Dick Bird took. It was embarrassing to see him such a coward, just as it had embarrassed Chip to see Bird gobble food that day in the draw. It was unseemly. It shamed him somehow, as if he were partly responsible for such meekness.

Then the roundup started, and there was a new railroad lining the country, with a new shipping point within twenty miles of Flying U Ranch. The Happy Family worked hard to get that first beef herd headed for Dry Lake and the brand new stockyard and shipping chutes. They almost forgot to devil Dickybird they were so busy thinking about the joys of a real railroad town. Even though it did contain only a store, a saloon, a hotel, and a blacksmith shop, it beat Cow Island. They could ship the steers and have a night to themselves.

So the Flying U roundup loaded out at Dry Lake one smoky September day, and camped a couple of miles out of town for the rest of that day and a night.

In the bed tent, men sat cross-legged on the ground with a bit of looking glass propped against an upraised knee, shaving as best they could under such unfavorable conditions. Between strokes they had to watch that no blundering foot kicked over their cups of lather, and that no hurrying cowboy heading for the doorway collided with the hand that wielded the razor.

Ordinarily they might not have bothered with such whole-sale primping, but there had been rumors of a dance in the hotel dining room that evening in honor of the arrival of the first roundup crew with the first shipment of beef to be loaded out at Dry Lake. It behooved the Flying U boys to do justice to the occasion.

Even Dickybird begged the loan of Weary Willie's razor and retreated to a far corner of the tent where he laboriously shaved that great pugnacious jaw of his. With a bluish cast to his skin where the black bristles stood thick below the surface, he emerged from the lather looking fiercer than before, but no one paid any attention to his looks any more. In that crowded tent, even the corners were at a premium, and Dick Bird's huge form was in the way. Men pushed and jostled him with identical oaths uttered in the identical tones they would have used in shoving a clumsy work horse over in a stall.

"Git over, can't yuh?" one would snarl at him. Or—"Move your big carcass!" and "Rattle your hocks outta the way, there!" With a meek persistency that rasped their patience, Dickybird moved himself as required and went on with his toilet. He wetted his black hair until it dripped, plastered it painstakingly down upon his right brow and back behind his ear in the accepted fashion. He shook out his neckerchief, folded it neatly, and retied it around his thick muscular neck. He dusted his shabby gray hat, set it carefully upon his head, and then, apparently unaware of his own ugliness, patiently waited for his turn at a broken piece of mirror that had been snatched away from him the minute he was through shaving.

Squatting just behind him with lather thick around his mouth, Cal Emmett poised his razor over his lip and slanted an exasperated glance up at Dickybird. "For cripes sake!" he cried. "If you don't git the hell outta here, I'll wring your damn' neck and feed yuh to the cat!"

"Why, sure," Dickybird placatingly answered, "I'm a-goin' right now." He laid the piece of mirror on a rolled bed and stood up, his hat crown grazing the ridgepole. Muttering an unintelligible insult under his stretched lip, Cal once more poised the razor as Dickybird started past. His leg brushed against Cal's elbow. Not much, but enough. The razor went high and sliced a neat little scale of flesh off the tip of Cal's nose.

With a yell of horrified astonishment, Cal heaved himself up and threw his cup of lather full into Dickybird's face. His language was scandalous. Those in the tent ducked out as if it were afire. They were certain that now even the timid giant would fight. But nothing like that happened. Instead, the tent flaps bulged and let out Dickybird on all fours, propelled by Cal's boot toe. While they stared, he picked himself up and started on a run for his horse, mopping lather from his face as he went.

With a disgusted oath Chip ran after him. "Here, hold on there, Dick! Come back here and knock the stuffin' outta Cal like he deserves!"

"I can't, Chip. I . . . I dassen't!" And with that unmanly confession, Dickybird spurred his horse into a run.

"Well, what d'yuh know about that!" Ted Culver ejaculated in an undertone, staring after him.

Cal came out with a finger pressed upon the bleeding cut

on his nose. "That there is the yallerest human I ever seen in my life," he declaimed loudly. "Yuh see me boost him outta there on the toe uh my boot? I'd 'a' bet money I'd 'a' got a rise out of him fer that, but . . . nothin' doin'."

"You'll get a rise out of me if you don't leave him alone," Chip cried hotly. "There's something the matter with Dick, or he'd have laid you out cold."

"Yeah, he's a damn' coward, that's what's the matter with him. He's yella," Cal retorted, still holding his nose.

"And you're a damn' sight yellower than he is, or you wouldn't bully a man who seems congenitally unfitted to defend himself," Chip told him bluntly as he swung into the saddle.

"And that oughta hold yuh for a while." Weary grinned at Cal as he, too, went for his horse. "Dickybird's congenitally unfit to defend himself. Remember that."

Such of the boys as were ready followed Chip and Weary, but they did not discuss the incident. One look at Chip's face was hint enough to shy around the subject. In Dry Lake, they saw Dickybird's horse tied to the hitch rail in front of the store, and they caught a glimpse of the man himself going into the saloon as they headed for the hotel. Already two couples were waltzing apathetically in the dining room, plainly visible through the uncurtained windows.

But the music was poor and there were not half enough girls to go around, and long before midnight the Happy Family adjourned to the saloon across the street. There at a small table against the wall, with a bottle and glass before him and a stranger opposite him, talking like a long lost friend, sat Dickybird. As they lined up at the bar, more than one of the boys glanced curiously that way. For one thing, they had never seen Dickybird take a drink of anything stronger than coffee, and the sight of him with a bottle was unusual enough to arrest their attention.

Furthermore, he looked oddly different. His hat was pushed back and his face was darkly flushed around his eyes. His big jaw looked uglier than ever. Whatever the whisky may have done to his wits, it certainly had not improved his looks any. He never was a talker, and he did not appear to be talking much now. He sat and scowled at the table, and now and then he nodded his head or spoke a word, evidently answering an occasional question.

For half an hour the room was rife with talk, laughter, the pleasant *clink* of glasses being filled and tilted together with a: "Here's lookin' at yuh," and a "Here's how!" Trouble rode other trails and left this place resting under the peace dove's wing.

Then Weary, who always shunned trouble as a matter of second nature—that is, within the bosom of the Happy Family—lifted a foaming mug of beer and, in the act of blowing the foam off the top, glanced beyond to the two at the table against the wall. He stared, nudged Chip's elbow, and gestured with his beer.

"Mama! Take a look at your chickadee over there, Chip. Look at 'im smile, would yuh? That sure must be a funny feller that's talkin' to him. I'd 'a' bet money there wouldn't nothin' on earth tickle Dickybird."

He meant those remarks for Chip's ears alone, but Cal Emmett, standing just beyond him, heard and turned to look. He gave a loud and insolent laugh.

"Yeah, he's smilin' now, all right, but I betcha all I got in my jeans that, if I was to walk over to'ards him, he'd jump out the window," he boasted.

Dickybird heard. Cal meant that he should hear. He lifted his glass and emptied it in one gulp, set it down, and pushed back his chair.

"Look it! What'd I tell yuh?" chortled Cal, throwing back his head to laugh. "You're goin' to lose a window, Rusty. . . ."

"When I throw the pieces of you through it," stated Dickybird in a slow, thoughtful mutter as he got up.

"Aw, dry up . . . you're drunk," snorted Cal, and turned his back, wanting to show how little he thought of the threat, as if Dickybird and anything he might say were beneath his notice.

Dickybird stood for an instant, teetering on his little high-heel boots. Deep set under his shaggy brows, his eyes glowed with a reddish light ominous to any who did not know the meekness of the man.

"Dick! Listen, Dick! Don't let yourself get worked up. . . ." On his feet beside him, the stranger plucked at his elbow, talking fast.

It was breath wasted. With an inarticulate snarl more beast than human, Dickybird lunged forward. With one drive of his huge paw, he slapped Ted Culver spinning across the room. Happy Jack he heaved over the bar headfirst into a row of bottles. While the rest of the boys stood slack-jawed, too stunned with amazement to move out of his way, he cuffed them aside and came at Cal Emmett standing there, goggling in plain unbelief of what he saw.

With one hand, he caught Cal by the throat. With the other, he clasped a shoulder. With the ferocity of a bulldog worrying a cat, he shook him. One strangled shriek of stark terror came from Cal's throat before those merciless fingers clamped down. After that, there was no sound from him save a horrible gurgle that ceased almost as soon as it began.

With an inhuman look of bloodlust on Dickybird's snarling face, and with inhuman strength, he lifted Cal and held him high in the air, pivoting on his little feet, his teeth showing in an animal grin under his big mustache. For ten seconds he stood there poised. Then with that horrible, beast-like snarl, he hurled Cal's senseless body upon the floor.

"Jump on him, boys! *Hold him!*" shouted the stranger, galvanized into speech and action. "He'll kill 'im . . . stomp 'im to death . . . he's done it before!"

The Happy Family did not wait to question; they rushed in between the demonic Dickybird and his kill. They grabbed his arms, and he flailed himself loose. They struck at his head, trying to knock him out—and there were fighters in the bunch. They never seemed to do more than graze him.

There was danger of their trampling Cal to death in their efforts to save his life. But Weary and Chip got him by the heels and dragged him out of the way, then carried him into Rusty's room at the rear, and laid him on the bed.

"Lock the door!" Chip panted, and went back to help if he could.

In the end, it was Chip who tamed the tornado. How, he himself did not know. Dickybird was for the moment free, standing against the wall with the Happy Family—as unhappy a group of cowboys as the state of Montana held at that moment—bunched and panting, waiting for his next move. Dickybird's red-flaming eyes were ranging from face to face as if he were choosing which one he would annihilate next. Chip, in reckless desperation, pushed through the line, and walked straight up to the demon. "Come on, Dick," he said quietly as he could, "let's hit the trail for camp."

The Happy Family held their breath, watching Dickybird. For the moment he seemed not to understand what Chip was saying. He stared at him fiercely, lifted a hand to clutch him, let it fall limply at his side. He dropped his head and stared at Chip's hand resting on his arm. They saw the demon go out of him. Saw the murder lust die out of his face, saw his eyes once more human. His shoulders sagged as his tense muscles relaxed.

He shivered as if a cold wind had struck him. "All right, Chip. Come on . . . le's go." His voice was husky, strained, as if the effort to speak was almost insuperable.

"You bet." Chip turned to the door, opened it. Like a man just awakened from a nightmare, Dickybird followed him, looking straight before him. "Looks like rain. Better button your coat, Dick." The door closed, and they were gone.

Inside the saloon, the stranger leaned over the bar, wiping the sweat of terror from his face while Rusty set out a bottle of something stronger than beer.

"My gosh, that was a close call for your friend," he exclaimed, shaking his head while he filled his glass with a hand none too steady. "Who's the damn' fool made that crack at Dick?"

"He was just joshin'," Shorty explained gruffly, taking the bottle as the stranger slid it toward him. "He didn't mean a thing in the world."

"Must be plain bug-house, then. Two men Dick Bird has killed . . . with his hands . . . *and his feet,* and for darn' sight less than what that feller said to him. What's the matter with you fellows? Didn't you know . . . ?" He paused to toss off the whisky.

"Never knew a thing about Dickybird gettin' like this. . . ."

"Dickybird? Hell! Dickybird! That what you been callin' him?" The stranger snorted. "How long has he stood for a name like that?"

"Oh-h, he never seemed to mind," Shorty parried the question uneasily. "He knew nobody meant anything outta the way. The boys is great joshers. He knows that. Or he oughta."

The stranger leaned an elbow on the bar and gazed pityingly at the rumpled Flying U boys. Again he shook his head with a baffled gesture. "Dick Bird," he informed them patiently, "has got the real stuff in him. More'n I ever would've believed. He's a boy I've known since I was a little shaver. Had a stepfather that used to tie him up and beat him . . . I won't go into details. But the neighbors bought in, and sent the stepfather to jail for the last stunt he pulled. He didn't get near long enough a sentence, though. Just a couple of years or so. He'd oughta got life.

"Dick growed up in them two years, seems like. He'd been took into a nice family and fed all he wanted to eat, and he shot up overnight, seems like. But he acted kinda queer. The old man had laid his head open with a club, that last time, and Dick never seemed to get over it altogether. Kinda slow and . . . well, humble is about the only word I can think of. Like as if he'd had all his nerve knocked out of him. The way he is now, I reckon.

"But I don't know . . . I guess it was just drove deep outta sight. His stepdad served his time, and come back into the country . . . come after Dick. Wanted to put him to work again on the ranch they had. Dick was big as a skinned horse goin' on sixteen, and I guess he looked like a good working proposition to the old man. The old lady was dead, and there was just them two in the family, yuh see." He stopped, started to roll a cigarette as if his story was finished.

Shorty exhaled a deep breath. "Did he go with the old devil?" he asked in his gruff way.

"Sure, he went. Never said a word, just moseyed right along." He paused while he struck a match on the edge of the bar and got his cigarette going.

"Hell!" snorted Jack Bates. "I don't see. . . ."

"You would, brother, if you'd been there. Dick went, all right. It just happened that I and another fellow didn't like the looks of things, and we rode over to the ranch about half an hour behind them two. We got there just in time to see the hull business. The old man had got off his horse, and turned it in the corral with the saddle on. Dick was pulling his saddle as we rode up. They never saw us a-tall. The old man had his quirt, and he walked up and hit Dick a belt over the head."

" 'I'll learn you to lie me into jail,' he says. And that was all he did say. Dick turned on him, and. . . ." The man hunched his shoulders. "Well, you saw about what would've happened to that mouthy friend of yours. I and this other fellow turned and rode off a little ways till Dick finished the job. The old man had it comin', and more, too. If he'd had the lives of a cat, I'd 'a' let Dick take every one of the nine same as he did the first one."

The Happy Family moved uneasily, avoiding one another's eyes.

"You said there was two," prompted Shorty.

The stranger lifted his glance from the glass he had been pushing absently back and forth on the bar. "Oh, yes . . . three, as a matter of fact. I didn't count a fellow Dick shot once, that had been runnin' him in a saloon. A bad actor, drunk, that come at Dick with a gun. Dick shot him. Nothing was ever done about that.

"But Dick's got the softest heart in the world, and he worried a lot over that killin'. Gave his gun away because, as he told me, once his temper gets away from him, he can't stop himself. He wants to kill whatever it is that has made him mad.

"But that other one . . . that was down on Powder River. Dick was punchin' cows for an outfit, and there was one big mouthed son-of-a-gun . . . he found out Dick would go a long ways and take 'most anything off a man, tryin' to side-step trouble. The loudmouth didn't know why, but he threwed it

30

into Dick every chance he got, and Dick took it all and never said a word back.

"But one night in town he took a few drinks, and this smart aleck started in on him." Again he bunched his shoulders. "It wound up same as tonight, only . . . that time, he wasn't pulled off in time. They had a kind of a trial, but everyone knew the fellow had it comin' to him, so they turned Dick loose."

He looked at them, twisted his lips in a sardonic grin, and refilled his glass.

"I don't know but what I'm to blame for this little outbreak tonight," he said slowly. "I was so tickled to see Dick, I set up the drinks. I didn't know he was nursin' a grudge against anybody. If I had, I sure wouldn't have steered him up against any liquor. Dick sure keeps a strangle hold on his temper as long as he's perfectly sober. But one drink's liable to touch him off if his feelings have been hurt. I sure am sorry, boys. I'd oughta thought."

"Oh, that's all right," Shorty hastily assured him, and looked up under his eyebrows at Cal who had staggered out of the back room and was leaning groggily against the bar, looking as if he had just come out of the tail end of a cyclone. "I guess maybe it was a good thing in the long run. Save trouble in the future."

"Well, I sure hope so. That young fellow he went away with can handle him all right, if he ever breaks out again. Dick's the kind that'll lay down his life for a friend. I could see he likes the kid. Tell him to kinda keep an eye on Dick and don't let anybody run on him, and he'll be all right."

So Shorty promised to deliver the message, and they had a drink and parted friends. Next day, a drizzling rain held the Flying U outfit idle in camp. Breakfast was late, but some of the boys were later. A few saddled and rode back into town with their slickers buttoned to their chins and their hats

pulled low. Those who didn't foregathered in the cook tent
where it was dry and warm, playing cards in a subdued way
and saying little to anyone. Dickybird sat hunched in a corner
mending his bridle when Cal came limping in, still looking
considerably the worse for wear. He got a cup of coffee and
was lifting a cold biscuit from a pan on the ground when
Dickybird rose from his place and came crouching forward
along the low tent wall.

Cal saw him and gave a squawk of terror. "Y-you leave me
alone! Don'cha come near me or I'll shoot!" He had dropped
the coffee and pulled his gun, aiming uncertainly, trying to
get Dickybird in line without jeopardizing the lives of Chip
and Weary who were behind him.

Dickybird stopped. "I . . . I only wanted to . . . kinda make
an apology," he said meekly. "I was drinkin' a little las' night,
I guess. I . . . never meant anything, Cal. Nothin' a-tall. I
guess I josh kinda hard when I . . . when I. . . ."

"Oh, that's all right, Dick," Cal said in honeyed tones of
warm friendship. "I josh too darn' hard myself, sometimes. I
. . . I don't want no hard feelin's between us, Dick. I . . . I sure
think a lot of yuh, Dick. I'd hate to have yuh think I. . . ."

"That's what I kep' tellin' Chip," Dickybird confided in a
relieved tone. "I told Chip you never meant nothin'. It was
just that I got t'drinkin', I guess. I been waitin' to apologize
fer las' night, 'fore I ride in to see my old friend, Lonnie
Henshaw. I wouldn't want no hard feelin's. Most generally I
can take a josh as good as anybody. But when I get to
drinkin'. . . ." He hesitated and looked appealingly at the
others. "Only for my pal Chip, here, I'm afraid I might 'a'
hurt somebuddy las' night."

"Oh, that's all right," quavered Cal, shrinking aside to let
Dickybird past him. "Don't mention it, Dick. I . . . guess I
had it comin'."

Dickybird stooped, awkwardly picked up the tin cup, and meekly handed it to Cal. "You spilled your coffee," he said mildly, and went out.

"Well, I'll be damned!" muttered Shorty under his breath, and gravely shuffled and dealt the cards.

From Hell to Kilpatrick's

For the May, 1906 issue of *Ainslee's Magazine*, the editor censored Bower's original title "From Hell to Kilpatrick's", substituting "The Girl from Kilpatrick's", but ignored a scandalous passage in which the woman is carried in a shocking but practical manner—back then, decent women kept their "limbs" and provocative ankles covered. A cowboy describes in authentic Montana range idiom his frightening odyssey involving the Rocking R, a real outfit east of the Bear Paws, and a young woman he finds afoot in the path of a roaring prairie fire. He also mentions "New Thought", one of Bertha's interests. She had experienced similar fires, and tapped her memory for other stories, most notably in LONESOME LAND (Little, Brown, 1912), and THE FLYING U'S LAST STAND, (Little, Brown 1915), two of her best novels.

Speaking uh the Rocking R outfit makes me think uh the deal that caused them to bid me a fond farewell—in other words, the time they canned me. It wasn't a square deal the way I sized it up. I was looking for a laurel wreath to set on my brow —and maybe a steady job as Family Hero, with nothing to do but look pretty and draw wages—and all I got out of it was my time and a lot uh disparaging remarks from the old man. If yuh want a man to admire your noble courage a lot, see to it that yuh don't hit his pocket. Just as sure as yuh cause him to lose a dollar by your heroism, he'll turn yuh down and call yuh hard names—all of which I learned at the Rocking R.

The way the play come up, I was breaking colts at the home ranch for fifty a month—only, I didn't get it. The old man was the sort that'll start yuh out on an errand today, and feel hurt if yuh don't get back bright and early yesterday morning. He'd say: "Here, Bill, saddle up and take this note to So-And-So, and bring me an answer before sundown," or something like that. And it didn't make any difference whether So-And-So was ten mile off or a hundred. Little Willie'd have to drift—and I will say that 'most generally Little Willie made good.

My top horse that summer was sure all right—when yuh once got on. But that same getting on wasn't any Labor Day picnic, either. Nobody but me could do any business with him at all, and even me, his beloved master, used to dance on one foot for upward of an hour with my other toe in the stirrup before there was anything doing. Then he'd eat up all the precious minutes he'd wasted in the first five miles, and I'd forgive him till next time I had to get on. It sure paid to do the lame chicken act with him—but Lord!—he was hard on the nerves, especially the old man's when he was burning with desire to see me start. The boys used to call me and Ring "the Human Telegraph", but Ring wasn't human—not quite. I named him Ring-Around-A-Rosey, but life was too short to use that cognomen common, so I called him just Ring, unless maybe on Sunday when I had time to burn.

I guess I'm a lot like Ring; it takes a lot uh prelude to get me headed anywhere, but I can go some, once I start. So here's the how:

The old man started me off one day—it was in the middle uh the shipping season—with a message for Blank Davis, the roundup boss. I was to get to camp by dark, change horses, and back to the ranch by daylight. The old man was in a sweat, and the "telegraph" had to get busy quick. It was some

35

hurry-up order about a shipment uh beef. The old man was grasping as a devil-fish, and it was frenzied finance, and then some, in shipping time.

So those being my orders and the old man being more pecky about it than usual, I saddled Ring and done the toe-dance, same as always. It was no good tying up a foot—that made him plumb ugly. The old man danced around and swore, and I danced around and done the same. Finally I got on, and the way we faded from view up the coulée must uh done the old man good to see. I had ninety miles to get over, but I could bank on Ring every time.

The way I was headed took me straight away from Willow Creek and over toward Sand Piper, but bearing more to the east, so as to strike the roundup somewhere along on Big Birch. You know what a dense population that country hasn't got. There ain't a ranch in twenty mile—nothing but the hills and coulées and benches, all wearing a large, loose garment uh pure lonesomeness.

So I was burning the earth, along about halfway across the flat between Square Butte and Hell Coulée—and that's sure as lonesome a land as ever I want to ride over—when I seen something white fluttering from what I took to be a sheep-herder's monument on the little pinnacle at the head of Hell Coulée; only there hadn't ever been a monument there before. I headed for the flag uh truce, though it was quite a bit out uh my way, and the old man hadn't give me none too much time to make the trip in, and it was getting along past the middle uh the afternoon then.

But out where nature hasn't ever been manhandled, it don't do to overlook any bets; in those places "All men are brothers" is a good rule to go by. I rode along, and pretty soon I seen it was some human waving me a come-on—and a little closer, I knew it for a woman.

Now, a woman is most generally a welcome sight to a man out on the range, where they ain't so thick not to be a novelty, but that's once when I wasn't glad to have one cross my trail. Woman means time wasted, always—and I hadn't none to throw away. I was plumb ignorant uh how she come there, or what was wrong, but I was willing to learn. She come running down to meet me, where it wasn't too steep; other places she was slipping and sliding down in the thick grass. You know how slippery grass can get.

When she got down where I was, I took a good look at her while I was lifting my hat. A fellow that's used to reading brands on sight, and all that, don't have to drop his jaw and gawk all day to size up anything. I couldn't place her, and I didn't know where was her home range, but I can say right here that she sure looked good to Little Willie! She was slim and light on her feet—I knowed her right there for a swell dancer, just the way she carried herself—and she had red hair—the dark, shiny kind that yuh like to watch the sun shine on, just to see it turn to gold. And her eyes put a crimp in me, right there.

They said things, those eyes did. They asked me please to be good, because she was in hard luck out there, and where did I come from, and what might my name be? And at the same time they was sassing me for being a strange man and on the earth at all, and for wanting to know things, and they double-dared me to think wrong, or to make a crooked move. I tell yuh right now, Little Willie's hands went up in the air, and he gentled right down till a lady could drive him—which she sure did.

She stopped twenty feet off, for all the world like a meadowlark that would like to make friends and dasn't. And I said—"Good afternoon."—just as if I'd met her in her dad's front door—wherever that might be.

That seemed to make her feel that we was on speaking terms, anyway, for she said: "Did you see anything of a loose saddle horse?"

I said I hadn't, and had she lost one? She told me she had—just as if it were a handkerchief, or as if she didn't realize that a saddle horse is trumps in a place like that. I've always thought that God made that country the last thing, and was kind uh sick uh the job, and slapped it together in a hurry, and never went back to smooth it down any.

So then she told me that she was Glen Kilpatrick, and was riding along to McHardie's place on Willow Creek. It's a good forty miles—some say it's only thirty-five, but they lie and the truth ain't in 'em—and she wasn't lost, because she'd often made the trip alone. But back there in Hell Coulée she'd got off to get a drink out uh the spring there, and her horse pulled out and left her afoot. She'd put a rock on the bridle reins, she said, but up jumped a jack rabbit and scared the horse, so he broke loose.

I said he'd probably head for home, and they'd be out looking for her, but it's a blamed discouraging place to find anyone in, and that's no dream. I didn't tell her that, but she didn't need any telling. She was wiser than me to the situation. She said the horse was a new one that her father had just bought off Frank Potter, so he'd take a straight shoot to Frank's place, which was down below the Rocking R—quite a piece. I hadn't run onto him—and you can see the prospect didn't cheer Glen Kilpatrick or me.

I set there and studied so hard my head ached, but I couldn't see out one thing to do. I couldn't take her up on Ring, nor she couldn't ride him alone, that was a cinch. She couldn't even get within ten feet of him but he'd back and snort, that impolite I was plumb ashamed of him. The walking wasn't all too up, as they say—there was miles of it in any direction you wanted, all up hill and down coulée. I figured that the closest place was her home—I knew where it was, but I'd never been right to the place—and that was a good long fifteen miles. I looked at her feet and shook my head without mentioning what I was thinking about, but she savvied, I guess, for her face got all pinky. There was no use taking after her horse—she said he'd been gone a couple uh hours. So I rolled me a cigarette and delivered my ultimatum.

I told her there was just the one thing for me to do, and that was to ride to her dad's and get another horse and bring it to her. She didn't look none hilarious, but she said it seemed the only way—if it wouldn't be too much trouble! There's one fundamental principle in life that none uh these New Thoughters or science sharps are ever going to argue away, and that is that nothing's too much trouble for a man when he's doing it for a woman—well, *the* woman. I'll bet Glen Kilpatrick was next to that great truth, too, the way her eyes laughed when she said it.

Then I looked at the place where I guessed the sun was, done some mental arithmetic with a page uh geography for the key, and did another thinking stunt. It would be plumb dark before I could get back even if I put Ring through all there was in him, and how was I going to find her again? If yuh know that country and how rough it is, with a dozen hills that look just alike, you'll savvy that I couldn't find her. Not in the dark—and it was going to be black as down a well at midnight. The air was heavy with smoke from prairie fires the sun couldn't drill a hole through, even. And as for the moon—well, there wouldn't be any till morning, anyhow.

I looked around for fuel, but there wasn't anything there, uh course. She said there was plenty uh currant bushes and the like down in the coulée behind the pinnacle. So I got off my horse and chowed him good—he'd stand with the reins dropped, all right, but I wasn't taking any chances just then—and we went down after some wood, so, when it got about time for me to get back, she could start a little fire on the pinnacle.

She was sure plucky, that little girl, and never made a whine about camping there alone for three or four hours. I know lots uh women that would 'a' cried at the mere mention uh such a thing.

Well, we packed up two loads apiece, and it was slow work. The hill was so steep we couldn't carry much at a time, and it was a heart-breaking climb, anyhow. I broke it up so she could feed a little at a time, and keep the fire going, if I was longer than we thought.

I gave up the last match I had—there wasn't but four—and commenced to play ring-around-a-rosey with that fool horse, and if ever I wanted to cuss and couldn't, it was right then. We'd spent quite a lot uh time getting the wood, and it was getting pretty late. I didn't want to leave that gritty little girl alone out there in the dark any longer than I had to—but Ring had to have his little fun with me, whether I had time to play or not.

When I did get on, I throwed the hooks into him pretty savage, and hollered—"See yuh later!"—to Glen. And my Adam's apple come up and like to choked me, so I had to swallow twice on it—the way she stood there by that little heap uh wood and watched me go, and tried to look as if she didn't mind being left. I wouldn't be afraid to bet she cried some out there on that pinnacle, when she couldn't see me no more. I don't mean that I'm so manly, but 'most anybody would look good to her out there.

I took my bearings by the hills, and hit her up pretty lively the first six miles or so. Lord, that's a rough bit uh land—about forty little draws and coulées to the mile, and some of them you can cross, and some you have to go around, unless yuh get off uh Ring—not on your life! I rode around the worst places.

I'd got six or seven miles, maybe, and was riding up the highest ridge of all—that one between Dry Fork and Sweet Grass Coulée—and it was getting dark already, but there was red in the sky, and a mighty rank odor uh burning grass. It was right in the prairie fire season, and the grass was heavy and fires common.

I got to the top, and glanced back over my shoulder—and, say, I could feel my hair stand on end under my hat. Straight across behind me stretched a line uh flame, from Willow Creek clear across to Sand Piper, and it was galloping up before a stiff southwest wind. Hell Coulée lay about in the middle of its path—and it wasn't going to do no turning out to go around, either! And that little girl back there on that pinnacle. . . .

I'll bet old Ring turned on a space you could cover with a dishpan—and back I put for Hell Coulée. Ring had his work cut out for him to reach her ahead uh that fire, and I was the boy that knew it, all right. I laid flat as I could, and sent him ahead all there was in him now, I'm telling yuh. You needn't ever tell me a horse hasn't got as much brains as a man; Ring knowed just as well as I did what was wrong. The brute in him told him to head the other way, and not to loiter, but the human in him told him about that little girl back there, and the human was a heap the strongest. He laid along the ground like a yellow streak, and went straight across places we'd dodged going out.

I'd 'a' said prayers, I guess, if me and Ring hadn't been so pressed for time. I watched that red glow in the sky now, I tell you! After I got down off that ridge I couldn't see the fire no more—and that made it forty times worse. I couldn't tell how

41

the game was going, and—say, a man can sure suffer a heap in a mighty short time, I found that out right then.

I guess we made a record run that time, all right. I know Ring never done anything like it before or since. After about a hundred and fifty years—according to the way I felt—we sighted the pinnacle. It wasn't dark then! The whole country looked like a tableau when the red fire is burning, and big flakes of burnt grass fell on us like a snowstorm done in black.

I seen her standing on the highest point, and I yelled, but I don't know if she heard me. The roar was like a fast train going over a bridge by that time. Anyway, Ring and me got there first, and it was blame' lucky we didn't have any farther to go, for Ring was about all in. He fair whistled going up that last hill.

I slid off beside her, and grinned, I was so tickled to be there. And she just put her arms around me for a second and never said a damn' word; she's got grit, that girl has!

I hollered for the matches, to set a backfire; but she'd used up the last one trying it. The wind blew so hard, she said, they went out fast as she could light them. Well, she'd done the best she could—she wasn't no cigarette fiend, and hadn't learned to keep matches going in an eighty-mile breeze. So that settled the backfire scheme, all right. The fire was galloping up the hill that fast we could feel it, and we looked like we was under a stage limelight—till the smoke rolled up onto us.

I didn't have no time to study what was best—I went to work. I tied Ring's bridle reins up and turned him loose, and he hiked. Then I grabbed the girl by an arm and put for Hell Coulée in a long lope.

The smoke come mighty near putting us both out uh business, and this story'd 'a' ended right there if it had. But we stayed with it and kept going, just 'cause we neither of us was particularly anxious to go out by the fire route. I'd noticed a slough-off down a piece from where we'd got the wood, where there was a kind of ledge part way down the coulée side, and around it just yellow clay and gravel. I made for that spot. I'll never tell yuh how we got to it and onto that ledge, but we did. I know, 'cause when I kinda come to myself and got the smoke out uh my lungs, we was both there. I've thought since that the Lord is mighty thoughtful. He must 'a' kept that place ready for us a good many years, so it would be there when we needed it worse than we'd ever needed anything before in our lives. I asked Glen about it afterward, and she sure agreed with me.

That fire struck Hell Coulée like a cyclone, and licked its chops around that off-slough, and like to broiled us with the heat; it would 'a', I guess, only it didn't last long. But while it did, Hell Coulée sure lived right up to its name and then some.

When it had passed—and, say, it made me think uh that piece uh poetry about "the hurricane had swept the glen"—I can't remember the rest—we just sat there and got our lungs full uh clean air once more, and rested, and we didn't say anything much. I guess we both felt kinda shaky to think what it was we'd gone up against. I know I did, and I was having a little prayer meeting inside about that ledge and one thing and another.

After a while the stars come out, and it wasn't quite so much like being several thousand feet down a coal mine, with no lamp. Then Glen said it didn't seem to do any good to set there like Micawber, waiting for something to turn up, and, if I was willing to tackle a little stroll of about fifteen miles, she was. I never knew Micawber—but I liked her grit, and I told her, if she thought she was good for fifteen miles, we'd strike out.

So we did. Anyhow, she said, we needn't be afraid of another prairie fire. You've been over burnt land, I guess. Did yuh ever walk across the prairie about forty minutes behind a fire? If yuh have, yuh know the kind uh deal we had. The ground didn't feel hot when we started; after a little, the warm began to get through our boots. And that rank, burnt-grass smell got plumb monotonous, and so did the black ashes flying up in our faces at nearly every step.

Before we'd got across the coulée I was sorry we started, for I could see it was going to be an even chance if she made it—and high-heeled boots ain't what I'd recommend for a walking match. I took my spurs off and hung them over my arm, and helped her along all I could—or all she'd let me. She started off mighty brave and independent, and wanted to walk fast, so as to get home before the supper got cold, it looked like.

But when a man has put in 'steen years on the range, and has gone up against every kind of scaly lay-out, and has nursed cattle through long, dry drives, he learns some things. I don't for a minute mean that Glen Kilpatrick was like cattle, but, all the same, I applied the same rules as far as I could. I made her take her time, and, when we came to a hill, or a nice pile uh rocks, I'd make her set down and rest. And when we came to water, she had to take a drink and bathe her face, and I done the same, for those ashes were a hard proposition now, I tell you.

Fifteen miles don't sound like such a terrible ways—and it ain't, when you're on a horse. But you start out and walk it. There is an old saying—you've heard it—"From Hell to Kilpatrick's". I never gave it much thought—but if it means Hell Coulée, I can tell yuh right now it's a mighty long jaunt. And you want to recollect that the fifteen miles meant straight across—an air line. It didn't count in all the hills we went down nor the ones we climbed to get across coulées. If we'd had one uh those clock businesses attached to us, I'll bet it would uh registered a good fifty miles—and that's no josh.

About halfway we came to a little creek. Glen was about all in, only she wouldn't own up. I made her set down and take off her boots and bathe her feet good. She kicked on doing it—but I went off a little way, and turned my back, and, anyway, it was pretty dark.

We stayed there quite a while and rested, and talked a little. We got pretty well acquainted on that trip. And I found out that she was The Woman, and always would be, but I didn't tell her so—not in so many words. I ain't quite a fool, I hope. But I do admire nerve, in man or woman; I never saw a coward that was much force, anyhow. You can't depend on them. And when yuh find a woman like Glen—well! I was singing "Just One Girl" down deep inside uh me before we left the ledge, even.

Then we went on, and history repeated itself till we was both plumb sick of it. It was walk, walk, walk—scramble and slide and fall down a hill—feel your way across a black coulée bottom, and watch out yuh don't tumble head-first into a washout. I went ahead, places like that, with one hand behind me holding to Glen—climb up out that coulée, walk, walk, walk—and so on, *ad infinitum*—if yuh know what that means. I don't, but it sounds like cuss words in a foreign tongue, so I guess it applies.

By and by, the moon peeked up over a mountain, like it wondered what the dickens was up, anyhow. And the land was dead still—no grass for the wind to whisper things to, and no living thing left to cheep at us and scurry away. Nothing but black, burnt prairie, till yuh felt like yuh was walking through the earth the next day after Resurrection, when the world had been rolled together and burnt. It got pretty chilly, too, along toward morning. I wanted Glen to take my coat and put it on, but she got mad at me mentioning it, so I had to work a scheme on her. I went along like I'd given up the idea —but I hadn't, not when I could feel her shiver every once in a while. So pretty soon I unbuttoned my coat and throwed it open, and said that walking was as warm work as wrassling calves. She eyed me suspicious, but I never let on. Then, after a while, I got hotter, and took my coat off, but I didn't offer it to her. I just slung it over my arm and walked on unconcerned.

After a mile or so I got tired uh carrying it, and said I guessed I'd leave it on the next big rock, and come after it in the morning, and then she walked into the trap and said, if I was going to leave it, she might as well put it on, for she did feel a little chilly! She was pretty sharp—but I hadn't tamed bronc's all these years for nothing!

The sun came up and found us still a-walking. We was closer to Kilpatrick's than we were to Hell Coulée, and that was about all I could see we had gained. But we kept pegging away, only we rested oftener, and Glen never objected. She looked like a tired little nigger, and I had to put my arm around her and help her along—which wasn't such a cross, either, only I did hate to see her so played out.

Then she got to the limit, where she couldn't go no farther, and didn't seem to care much whether she ever got home or not. It ain't only freezing and seasickness that puts yuh into that frame uh mind; yuh can just get so tired you lay 'em down and don't give a cuss.

So I had to carry her that last mile or so. I took her on my back, which wasn't graceful nor picturesque, maybe, but it was practical. Yuh can't carry a woman very far in your arms, the way they do on the stage; it looks better, but you wouldn't get far.

When we did get down into Kilpatrick's coulée, Glen

roused up and walked the last few hundred yards, and we went up to the door, and I knocked. Old Kilpatrick come to the door, and, so help me, he didn't know Glen from a hole in the ground, she was that black and draggled, and with my coat on. She had to call him by name, and he looked kind uh dazed even then—and I can't say I blamed him any. But I would 'a' felt plumb jealous at the way he gathered her into his arms, if he hadn't been her dad.

We had something to eat, and then Little Willie slept the clock around twice, more or less. Then I felt more normal—except in the region uh my heart—and I borrowed a horse from Kilpatrick and went and delivered that message to Blank Davis, only they'd moved twice away from Big Birch, and I had a dickens of a time finding camp, and rode about a hundred and twenty-five miles.

I delivered it, all right—trust Little Willie for that!—and hiked back to the Rocking R only about two days overdue. And that's where I got turned down. Ring had gone back—how he dodged the fire's a plumb mystery to me, but I told yuh Ring was half human—and the old man wanted explanations and then some. I told him all about how the play come up, and waited for the congratulations. If anybody should ask yuh, I'm still a-waiting! It was just my luck that he hates old Kilpatrick worse than snakes, and by my courage and chivalry—he had some different names for it, which I won't repeat in public—I'd caused him to lose a rise in the market, or some darned thing. He was dollars to the bad, anyway, and so Little Willie had to drift.

But I ain't worrying none. I went straight back over to Kilpatrick's and went to work for him, and he's a grateful old party. He's going to let me marry Glen—which shows how sensible he is, because I'd marry her anyway, whether he let me or not.

The Sheepherder

This simple early story, which appeared in *Ainslee's Magazine* (1/05), presents a dramatic confrontation during a deadly Montana blizzard. Strong sensory details bring the story to vivid life, one of B. M. Bower's hallmarks. At a lonely cabin, a hungry dog's actions establish the story's mood as a sheepherder vainly seeks safety for his flock. He and his charges barely survive the bitter night. By the time it was in print, Bertha had left Clayton Bower, and filed for divorce. If he was the model for the brother, her reasons for decamping are clear. Animals had prominent rôles in later stories: a psychic pinto cat increased the mystery in THE VOICE AT JOHNNYWATER (Little, Brown, 1923), and THE PARAWAN BONANZA (Little, Brown 1923) features a pet turtle and a garrulous parrot modeled after a real pest of a bird at Bower's Nevada mine camp.

Mack shivered on the doorstep, his muzzle pressed close against a narrow crack in the door. He quit snuffing lustfully at the smell of frying bacon long enough to cock one ear at the swirl behind him. The breathless swish of wind-driven snow was all about him. He listened a moment and turned, whining, to the crack again.

He hated the cold and the bitter drive of the storm, and he was hungry with the hunger that comes to growing dogs and children. He could hear Dot setting the table, and he could smell the coffee boiling—not that he cared for the coffee, however. It was the bacon—and the warm boards behind the stove, just under the reservoir, where he could curl up and sleep—and it was Dot with her soft hands patting his sleek black head and making believe at pulling his ears. When Mike was gone, he was not shut out like this to freeze, and he was not kicked cruelly in the ribs, either. He hated Mike, and he hated Mike's big overshoes that were at this very minute lying in his favorite place under the reservoir, making the boards nasty and wet with melting snow. If Mike were a dog. . . .

Surely there was something back there in the storm. Mack stopped whining, listened, shook the snow off his back, and rushed out to the gate, barking loudly. There he waited, *bow-wowing* hysterically, keeping one eye on the door behind him.

In a moment the knob turned, and Mike's tousled head appeared in a jealously meager opening, while the warmth of the kitchen, doing battle with the cold from without, enveloped his head and shoulders in a white haze.

"C'm back here, you fool, you! C'm 'ere!"

Mack only barked the louder.

And then even Mike's dull ears heard alien sounds—the *yelp, yelp* of sheep dogs and the confused murmur of many animals.

A shape took form beyond the gate, and a voice greeted Mack, who subsided after a querulous growl or two that he should have made such a mistake.

"Hello! C'm in, whoever yuh be!" called Mike, and opened the door wider. Mack, trying to sneak in unnoticed behind the stranger, got another kick for his pains, and retired to nurse his wrath and his ribs in the coal shed.

Mike shut the door and cursed the cold. "Oh, it's you, Joe! Come up t' the fire and thaw out. Didn't walk, did yuh?"

"Thanky, Mike. I can't stop. My sheep's out here. I just stopped t' get located, for I was plumb lost. I seen the light, but I couldn't tell whose 'twas."

"Sheep driftin', hey? Hope they pile over a cutbank, some'ers. Supper's about ready, ain't it, Dot? You warm up a little, and then we'll eat."

A fair-haired girl in a blue dress and checked apron was kneeling at the farther side of the stove, taking something from the oven. The man looked again and saw it was biscuits—long rows of biscuits in a pan, with crusty, light brown tops and a delicious smell.

"Why, Joe Porter! You sure have drifted off your range, haven't you? You're just in time . . . supper's ready, and I guess there's plenty of it."

She smiled at him, showing him three dimples and a row of pretty teeth—surely an unfair array of weapons to flash before a weary man's face. And the biscuits—and the bacon. He smiled back at her, but shook his head regretfully.

"It looks good, all right, but I can't stop. The dogs can hold the sheep t'gether for a few minutes, but I can't stay t' supper. The river ain't fenced down here in your field, is it, Mike?"

"You still herdin' fer Taylor?" Mike's face took on a crafty smile. He hated Taylor, and he hated Taylor's sheep. He stopped just short of hating Taylor's herder as well. "Man, you're crazy t' follow them fool sheep on a night like this. They'll stay in the field, likely. My line fence is good . . . it'll hold 'em. Set down and take off them overshoes and git yer feet in the oven."

"Is the river fenced?" persisted Joe.

Mike moved the coffee pot from the back of the stove to the hearth, where the steam of it smote the herder's nostrils, and his empty stomach yearned after it.

"Aw, never mind the river . . . come and eat yer supper. If yuh want t' commit soocide, they's easier ways than freezin'."

"I'll have t' go . . . much obliged, Mike. I couldn't get 'em

home against this storm, so I'll just have t' stay with 'em.
There ain't . . . could I get 'em in a corral or some place for
the night, Mike?"

"Naw, yuh couldn't. I ain't got no shelter for Taylor's
sheep. You can turn 'em loose in the field and let 'em take
their chances, seein' they're here. An' you're welcome t' stay
here, with a good supper an' a good bed . . . I ain't got any
quarrel with you."

Dot had poured a cup of coffee, trickled a thin stream of
canned cream into it, and added sugar. "Here, Joe, you drink
this, anyway. It'll warm you up. You better stay. A man's
worth more than a bunch of sheep."

Joe took off a mitten, and emptied the cup in two great
gulps.

"That's sure all right, Miss Hawkins, thanks. I'd like t'
stay, all right. I ain't stuck on blizzards . . . but I can't leave
them poor animals t' face it alone."

He pulled the door open and listened, then closed it again,
and set his broad back against it. The dogs were holding the
sheep, he could tell by the sound. He could afford to steal
another minute of light and warmth and of being in Dot's
presence.

"Oh, here's that song yuh wanted, Miss Hawkins," he
said, fumbling inside his overcoat. "I copied it off last night. I
hope yuh can make it out. It's all there, I guess."

Dot took the paper, written closely with lead pencil, and
slipped it into her pocket. Then she held out a paper bag,
warm and moist from the hot biscuits and bacon it held.

"Take this along, Joe. It'll come in handy, maybe. Oh, it's
just to pay for the song, so don't say anything. I'm awfully
obliged."

Joe looked wistfully around the shabby little room and at
the face of the girl. "Well, I must get moving. Good bye."

"Good bye," repeated Dot, her eyes misty. "Good luck."

"So long, Mike," added Joe cheerfully.

The door slammed, shutting out the wind and snow and the cold, shutting out the tall form of the sheepherder as well. Mike lifted the lid of the stove, laid in a lump of coal, dragged his chair across the floor to the table, and took up knife and fork.

"What'd you want t' give him all the biscuits fur?" he growled. "A fool like that ought t' go hungry . . . and freeze, too."

"I didn't," retorted his sister calmly. "There's plenty left. He ain't a fool, either. He's what I call a brave man."

"He's what I call a darned fool," reiterated Mike sullenly.

Dot crumpled the paper in her pocket and listened, shuddering, to the wind.

Out in the field where the world seemed but a dizzying dance of frozen white meal, Joe plodded steadily against the wind, guided by the staccato barking of his dogs. The sheep huddled together, their wizened, reproachful little faces turned from the cruel beat of the blizzard.

Joe took his station behind them and, once his face was sheltered, set his teeth greedily into the crusty warmth of a biscuit. He had eaten breakfast before day, had munched a chunk of sourdough bread with a cold slice of bacon at noon, and had drunk from a brackish spring. Then the blizzard had swept down upon him before he could reach shelter, and the sheep refused to face into it toward home, and he had walked and shouted and cursed the shivering, drifting blot of gray. They had wandered blindly until now.

Joe thrust his bare fingers into the bag and counted the biscuits. Two—three—four—there had been five—light, fluffy things such as only a woman can make. He caressed them each in turn. The warmth of them—and the smell—and the crisp, sweet bacon between!

Only a healthy man who had walked long hours in the cold may know the keen agony of hunger, or the ecstasy of yearning at the whiff of fresh fried bacon. The fingers closed around a biscuit.

"Oh-h, Bonnie!"

A dog's voice, a tired, patient voice, answered, away to the right. He could hear her scurry toward him, and he knew the trustful shine in her eyes even though he could not see it.

The little creature bounded against his legs and whimpered pitifully. Joe stooped in the snow and patted her eager little head.

"It's ladies first, ain't it, Bonnie, old girl? Ain't that the stuff? Yuh wasn't looking for no such hand-out as that, out here in this frozen hell where the freeze is ground up into flour and throwed in your face, hey? Naw, it's a cinch yuh wasn't. That went down easy, didn't it? Here's another, old lady . . . put it away where it'll do the most good. They're out uh sight, them biscuits are, Bonnie, cause . . . Dottie made 'em!"

It seemed that even the dog read the wistfulness of the last whispered words, for she raised her cold muzzle against the man's chilled, brown cheek, and whined. Joe pushed her gently from him and stood up.

"That's all, Bonnie. Lad's got t' work, too, this night, and he's going t' have a taste. There, now . . . go on . . . 'way round 'em!"

The dog gave a short, shrill *yelp* that held more of courage and not so much of weariness, and bounded away into the blur.

Joe listened until he heard her driving in the stragglers on the far side of the band. Then he sang out cheerfully: "Hi, Laddie!"

From the left came a glad *yelp* and another dog wallowed up to the master and crouched, fawning, at his feet. As before, Joe stooped and greeted him like a comrade.

"Good boy! You're sure the proper stuff, Lad. And what d'yuh think, say? Here's your supper, all hot from the stove. Ain't that the clear article? Say, Lad, how's your appetite for warm biscuits, hey? Set your teeth into that once and tell us what yuh think. Ain't it a peach? You're sure the lad that can appreciate good grub on a cold stand like this . . . you bet. If you'd 'a' seen her, Lad, with the lamp a-shining on 'er hair, and in her eyes when she handed these out t' me, you'd love her, Lad . . . you sure would. No, there ain't any more . . . I took one myself . . . it was an odd one, yuh see. I just had to, it smelled so good . . . and she made it. Well, lick my fingers, then. I wish I hadn't eat that other one, Lad . . . on my soul I do. I was a big chump, that's what. There . . . go back and keep 'em close . . . go on!"

The dog ran back to his post, and the man sighed, folded the paper bag as best he could, and put it tenderly away inside his coat before he followed after his sheep. Tramping blindly with the wind at his back, he pictured the little room he had left behind. He smelled the coffee boiling, and heard the rattle of the dishes while they ate. He felt the warmth, even while he thrashed his body with his arms to fight off the creeping numbness in his hands. He tried to forget the gnawing hunger while he hummed the song he had penciled so painstakingly the night before, in the little cabin where he lived alone with his friends, the dogs.

"There's a sob on every breeze. . . . There sure is, all right, on this one. What's the matter, Bonnie? Why, damn it, it's the river . . . and no fence!"

He set off at a run toward Bonnie, raging at her charges and trying all she could to turn them. Stumbling, breathless, slipping on the wiry sand grass which bordered the river, Joe reached her and heard the rush of water close below—too close.

He whistled imperiously to Lad, who all unconscious, was pressing the band nearer to the death that waited a scant two rods away. Lad came with a rush, and together they charged the bunch desperately. It was hard work in the face of that gale, and by the time they were safe, away from that treacherous, overhanging bank, Joe felt almost warm.

Then the dreary march began again. Mike Hawkins's south fence held them for a few minutes, but it had only three wires, and they were not the tightest, and the sheep crawled under, leaving whole handfuls of wool to gather snow and swing on the barbs. Beyond there was no river, but there were dangerous washouts where the surrounding country drained into coulées.

Into one of these the sheep drifted, and like gray troubled waters, followed its windings to its outlet in the coulée. Then, worn with travel and pinched with cold, they halted at last under a high rock bank and crowded close for warmth, while the wind passed harmlessly over their heads to the hillside beyond, and only the snow sifted silently down upon their cowering backs.

The dogs lay down at the outer edge of the flock, and licked their chilled feet while they rested. Their master tramped up and down beside them, beating his hands to keep the blood moving and thinking of many things.

He wondered how a man felt who could refuse to shelter suffering brutes on such a night because of a prejudice against their owner, and calmly allow a comrade to face that wilderness of cold, also because of that prejudice. He wondered if Dot read the song he had given her, and if she noticed the smudges where he erased words not spelled at first to his liking. He wondered if the coffee pot still stood on the stove, with the coffee hot and strong and fragrant.

What a bitter thing is a blizzard—a blizzard at night. How the cold eats up a man's courage and grips at his blood, chilling it even as it bubbles fresh from his heart. Why hadn't he left the sheep? What was it Dot had said? *A man is worth more than a bunch of sheep.* Well, yes. But is a man worth more than his honor?

What if he had left them? No one could blame him, surely —no one, that is, except himself—and—yes, Dot. She knew he would not stay, else why did she pour that cup of coffee? Coffee? What wouldn't he give for a cup now? Yes, and one of those biscuits.

Br-r-r, but the cold could bite! There would be a loss among the sheep—the weak ones couldn't stand a night like this. It was tough enough on the strong. Was that a coyote? What business had even a coyote out on such a night?

For comfort, he turned to his dogs. "Bonnie, old girl, this is sure hard lines, ain't it? I'd set down and let you snuggle ag'in' me and get warm, if I durst. It's mighty little warmth you'd get, though. I ain't running no furnace heat at the present time, old lady, I tell yuh that. How's it coming, Lad? Think they'll find us when it lets up, hey? I'd hate t' have any money up on it, wouldn't you? But we ain't all in yet, you bet your life we ain't. Our paws don't go in the air just so long's they can wiggle-waggle . . . ain't that right?

"Gee, Bonnie, I wish't I could lick my paws and get some feel into 'em! I wish't I could get hold of her little paws . . . they're soft an' warm . . . that warm yuh can feel 'em clear to your toes, Lad. That's right. Yuh can."

When day sifted through the snow clouds, the storm had not lifted, although it raged less fiercely.

56

Dot cleared away the breakfast feverishly, and swept the kitchen with less care for the dust under the stove and in the corners than was usual to her methodical nature. Mike toasted his feet in the oven and smoked.

"There's five calves missin'," he grumbled. "Drifted off when the blizzard struck yist'day. I wish't it'd clear off so'st I c'd go and look fur 'em."

"I'll go," volunteered Dot eagerly. "I don't mind the storm a bit. I think it's fun to ride in it."

Mike sucked on his pipe and grunted. "Anything's fun that yuh don't have t' do. If yuh go, yuh want t' fix fur it. This ain't no day for women's skirts a-floppin' on a side-saddle. You go like a man, if yuh go at all. Put on my chaps an' fur coat."

Having eased his conscience, he dropped his lank body back to the heat and prepared for a comfortable forenoon, at least.

Dot put on the masculine attire and made other strange preparations for hunting stray calves. For one thing, she took a pint flask and filled it nearly full of strong black coffee, stole into Mike's room, and finished filling it from his jug of brandy, then corked it tightly and slipped it into a pocket in the fur overcoat.

"Has the wind changed since last night?" she asked when she was ready, with only her eyes to show who she was.

"Nah. Ain't likely to, either," grunted Mike.

Outside, she called Mack and waded awkwardly in her strange garb to the barn, where she saddled not one horse, but two. Mike had not even offered to saddle up for her, and it took some time, cumbered as she was by the heavy coat. She wondered as she struggled into the saddle how men managed to carry so many clothes? She was stifled with heat as she rode away to the south.

Following the line fence, she discovered the place where many ragged little white bunches swayed on the lower wire, and rolled precipitately off her pony.

With the hammer she had stuck in her pocket for just such an emergency, she deliberately pulled staples, the number of which would have wrung the soul of Mike had he seen her. When the wires lay flat, she led the horses over them, mounted, and rode on before the wind.

A mile of straight level, then came the broken ground where the washouts lay. She stopped, called Mack to her, and held something down for him to smell—a folded white paper, covered with penciled writing.

"Seek him, Mack!"

It was the tall fellow who never kicked a dog, but always had time for a pleasant greeting, and who followed sheep around the country. It was perfectly simple. To find him, one had only to find the sheep—and did not the odor of many sheep cry aloud to the very heavens? Seek him? It was a joke. Down this washout, for instance, the air was rank of sheep. A little farther, now. . . .

Dot rode up to the shivering gray patch under the bank, where two weary dogs stood guard, and a wearier man stumbled back and forth along a pitiful, black-beaten trail.

He eyed her stupidly, still staggering along the path he had made. "Hello!" he said, as one half-wakened from sleep. "Are yuh . . . looking . . . f'r someone?"

"I'm looking for you, Joe." Dot choked and swallowed hard.

Joe lurched nearer, studying her figure wonderingly. "Dotty . . . is it . . . you? I'm . . . about all in, my girl."

"No, you ain't, either," cried Dot fiercely, tearing open her coat. "A man like you . . . to keep your feet and your wits all night . . . you ain't going to give up now. I never slept for

58

thinking of you in the storm. Here, drink this, and then climb onto Mike's horse. Here, it will steady you."

Joe lifted a wooden hand, and dropped it again, with the shadow of a smile. "Can't, Dot. My hands . . . they're snowed under, yuh see."

Dot tore at the cork with her teeth. "Here, Joe . . . lean against me . . . that way. I'll hold the bottle. Drink it all . . . every drop. There's brandy in it . . . I stole some of Mike's."

When Joe spoke again, his voice was firmer. The light came into his eyes. "You're the proper stuff, little girl. A little more and I'd 'a' been all in. I can't climb into that saddle . . . I'm limber as a froze jack rabbit . . . that's what."

So Dot got down, and helped him while the horse, that was used to having Mike boosted into the saddle in the gray of a morning, waited decorously till they were quite ready.

"I'll send Mike after someone for the sheep. A man's life comes first . . . yours does, Joe. Mother'll be home t'day, and she's as good as forty doctors. You'll stop with us till you're well."

Joe steadied himself in the saddle, although he could not hold the reins with his frozen fingers.

"Come, Lad," he said huskily. "Come, Bonnie, my girl. Yuh mind them biscuits yuh had? You'll get some more just like 'em, maybe. We're going t' heaven, sure. We're going . . . home . . . with Dottie."

The Vanguard of the Philistines

The *Ainslee's* editor didn't like the title Bower had chosen for this story, either, and substituted "Happy Heart, Cowboy". It appeared in the April issue in 1905. The light-hearted analogy with the ancient Biblical conflict pits cattlemen who first came to Montana's open range against homesteaders' barbed wire and aggressive attitudes. A clever cowboy involves the local schoolma'am in getting up a dance to divert a stout Irish widow and her rancorous sons while the "Philistines" get their beef herd across the river. The cowboy's buddy, Beetle, delays the "Israelites" further with a confusing trick adopted from real life. Cherubic but scrappy, Beetle was the prototype for Flying U character Pink Perkins, who first appeared in print in "Rowdy of the Cross L" in the *The Popular Magazine* (5/06).

Today the old enmities are gone. Now rancher-farmers run cattle on the lush, grassy hay meadows and raise grain instead of Cain up on the arid benches. Hannahan pulled up just where the trail whipped around a huddle of rocks and dipped unexpectedly into the valley of the Chiquita, and made him a smoke in the inattentive manner which bespeaks a mind steeped in meditation.

The hills beyond showed yellow in the warm haze of Indian summer. Heat waves set the air aglimmer and drew one's senses into waking dreams. Hannahan, however, was not dreaming—his gaze was too direct and purposeful for that. He studied the level land below as though he were playing chess and the valley was the chessboard.

Chiquita Valley was a stockman's paradise, harnessed to the plow of the small farmer. The thick prairie sod was carved into gray-brown fields, with the sweet, rich grasses buried under four inches of fertile soil. Where the wild range cattle had wandered at will, long lines of wire fencing checked the land into tilled squares jealously guarded by narrow lanes.

Hannahan drew a match along his stamped saddle skirt, cupped his hands abstractedly, and followed the trail with his eyes to where it was gashed by the unquiet blue of the river, and beyond to where it showed a brown band against the yellow crispness of the hillside.

Chinto lifted a front hoof tentatively, got no encouragement from his master to proceed, and planted it pettishly into the flour-fine dust. He swung his head and looked back reproachfully, his ears pointing different ways. He was warm and weary, and he thirsted for the cool swash of river water down his throat. But Hannahan did not move except to empty his lungs of smoke, and the horse sighed heavily and waited. After a minute the ear that pointed down the hill twitched to attention; the other gave over listening for Hannahan's throat-chirp, and leaned forward, listening. The animal's eyes stared alertly at the jumble of rocks that hid the trail, and Hannahan, warned instinctively by the tense ears, brought his eyes and his thoughts up from the valley and listened, also.

A girl rode leisurely around the rocks, at first glanced indifferently at the horse and rider, and then with some interest. Hannahan was conscious of a sudden warmth in his chest; his gray hat went up off his forehead.

"Good morning," he said. "You aren't going to pass up an old friend, I hope?"

"If it isn't Mister Hannahan . . . Hannahan of the Happy

61

Heart! What mischief is in the air now? You're getting rather close to the land of the Israelites . . . for a Philistine."

"Aw, don't go calling names, Miss Conrad. I guess I am standing with my front feet over the deadline, all right . . . what of it?"

"You know how we don't love cowboys down there." She waved her hand airily at the valley below.

"Are yuh giving that out for a personal opinion?" Hannahan threw away his cigarette.

"I was speaking for the Israelites. They're just praying for a chance at some of you. They mean to slay and spare not."

"That there's a prayer that's soon answered . . . me being a direct answer to prayer." His tone was unalarmed.

Miss Conrad laughed. "Better not cross the line. If it's the ford, it won't do you a particle of good. They are watching it rather closely, and they are still highly indignant over the last time."

"What last time? The Big AJ hasn't made a move toward it yet this year."

"Some other outfit did, though . . . and the Israelites never discriminate when cattlemen are concerned. A large herd came down the lane one Sunday afternoon, and were so inconsiderate as to meet William McKinley Roosevelt Jones on his bike."

"The name stampeded the bunch, I reckon."

"Something did. William McKinley Roosevelt Jones turned out for them, but not soon enough. The herd turned out, also . . . 'way out, through old man Hadley's wheat field, and from there into the garden of the Widow McCoy. Did you ever meet the Widow McCoy, Mister Hannahan?"

"No, but I've heard tell of her." Hannahan grinned. "She's got a temper and a boy, hasn't she?"

"Yes, and opinions differ as to which is the worst . . . only she has two boys and only one temper. The boys divide their time between watching the trail for cattle, and praying to be led into temptation. I really think, Mister Hannahan, you'd better not go down."

"I wonder if I'd look tempting to them," Hannahan mused, rolling another cigarette daintily between his fingers. "You haven't explained yet how it comes you are ranging down on the Chiquita," he remarked.

"I'm teaching their school. I couldn't get another so near home, and the salary is good."

Hannahan sighed. "The things people will do for money! Look at me, scouting around a bunch of measly grangers. . . ."

"Then it is the ford?"

"You can just bet it's the ford. We've got twelve hundred fat steers on the trail, with cars ordered at Chinook for day after tomorrow. Sure it's the ford, all right . . . and it's those sons-uh-toil to the woods if they try to stop us."

"There's no *if* about it. Someone is always on the watch ready to warn the whole valley, and their crops are mostly gathered, so there's nothing but fences for a stampede to demolish."

Hannahan lifted a square, expressive shoulder. "That's a county road down there, and the Big AJ isn't an outfit that's going to be bluffed out of a game by any bunch of long-eared Mormons."

Miss Conrad regarded him with serious, sympathetic eyes. "The lane is county road, certainly, but the ford is in the middle of a quarter section owned by the Widow McCoy."

Hannahan let his lids droop, and Miss Conrad recognized the sign; it meant that forty Widow McCoys could not dismay Hannahan of the Happy Heart.

"How will you manage it?" she asked, not doubting that he

would somehow accomplish the job.

"Search me," Hannahan said cheerfully. "But you can gamble we're not going to make any forty-mile drive with no water, taking that bunch uh longhorns around by Wood's ford. Besides, the cars will be there day after tomorrow . . . and so will the Big AJ. Old Jimmy Knauss 'most generally wins out, when he makes up his mind to."

Miss Conrad looked thoughtfully down into the peaceful valley. "They do have such a bitter enmity against stockmen," she remarked. "And they love to fight better than anything else . . . unless it's dancing."

"That's me," Hannahan observed.

"If there were only a dance in the valley . . . ," she mused.

"Well," he demanded, "why can't there be one?"

"Tonight? That's very short notice, and there's no music nearer than Lazy Trail, and that's abominable."

"Well," said Hannahan, "if you can get the rubes rounded up, I'll fix the music. We've got a couple of fellows in the outfit that can thump thunder out of a guitar and mandolin."

Miss Conrad's eyes got sparkles in them. The droop of Hannahan's lids grew more pronounced.

"Think we can make it?" There was a dare in his voice and eyes.

"I think so . . . this is Saturday, you see, and early. If we can think of some plausible reason for launching a couple of unknown musicians upon the valley without warning . . . are you sure that they are unknown?"

"Dead certain. We was talking about this lay-out down here, last night." Hannahan slid over in the saddle to rest himself, and meditated. When Hannahan did that, obstacles had a way of melting like snow in a Chinook. "Say! I'm your dear cousin Jack," he soon announced.

Miss Conrad opened her eyes and smiled skeptically.

"Beetle's another cousin, and Parrot Jim is our sidekicker. We're just riding through the country looking for a ranch" —Hannahan made a wry face when he said it—"and we call on you at your boarding place. You can easy persuade us to stay a while, and you can ask the neighbors in for a little sociable dance, see? How do yuh like the way that stacks up?"

Miss Conrad still looked skeptical. "It's rather embarrassing," she demurred, "to adopt offhand a cousin who is known to have a weird attraction for adventures . . . misadventures, I might say . . . let alone a cousin I never so much as heard of before, called Beetle. Beetles," she finished dismally, "are my especial horror."

"This one's sure OK," Hannahan assured her. "You'll like him, all right enough . . . everybody does. He's just a kid-looking fellow anyway, with dimples and blue eyes and a soft little voice. You'd almost take him for a girl dressed up in cowboy togs. But he's there with the goods, all right . . . a broncho-fighter, and the most surprising little devil that ever wore chaps. He can carry the thing through. I'll back Beetle with all the dough I've got."

Miss Conrad gave him a queer sidelong look. "He'll have his work cut out for him, as you cowboys say. I board with the Widow McCoy."

"The dickens yuh say!" Hannahan instinctively slid straight in the saddle. The Widow McCoy had a spectacular record for defending her own, and her name was spread abroad in the land.

"Could you come in time for dinner?" she suggested.

Hannahan wrinkled his nose at the sun and considered. "Would we stand any show? Beetle hates like the mischief to miss his regular feed."

Miss Conrad reassured him the Widow McCoy also held the proud distinction of being the best cook in the valley, and was never more pleased than when strangers rode hungry to her door. "The only danger," Miss Conrad added, "is that you may suffer from acute indigestion, induced by overindulgence."

Hannahan's face spoke admiration. "Say, you and Parrot would make a pair to draw to, for language. The things he can do to his mother tongue would make a prairie dog sit up and take notice."

Miss Conrad's lips drew together. "I must confess I can't quite see the connection. . . ."

"That was a compliment, only I forgot to stick the label on. Parrot is educated, let me tell yuh. He was close-herded through Princeton . . . or some other knowledge factory. Anyway, the brand of learning he's got is about as good as there is. He don't talk more than once a year or so . . . that's why they call him Parrot . . . but when he does gets strung out, it's the clear article. He can sure sing, too. I'd rather listen to him on night guard than go to the best show yuh can name. I'll get him to sing for yuh, if I can."

"I have a mandolin," Miss Conrad observed, "and Bud McCoy has a fine guitar. His mother got it for his birthday. He can't find the same string twice, but Missus McCoy thinks it looks 'toney' tied with a big red bow and hung over the sofa. Bud also has a pugilistic temperament, and an echo in his brother, Patsy. Bud does the fighting, and Patsy does the threatening. You needn't mind Patsy at all . . . but keep an eye on Bud."

Hannahan's lids drooped again, and he smiled quietly to himself. "I'll put the boys next," he promised, "and much obliged to you. Say! Beetle's got a reputation trailing behind him like a comet on a dark night. You better call him something else. Call him . . . well, call him Eddie. He looks the part, all right, but it'll most likely make him grit his teeth.

We'll get along about noon . . . and the Big AJ'll sure be grateful to you, Miss Conrad, for helping 'em out. Fact is, I know of a dandy little pinto that'd be a swell lady's horse, and it's safe t' say he's liable to meet that same fate if this thing goes through. It's got t' go through. The Big AJ will be down to cases for cars if we don't make Chinook on time. Cars are mighty scarce this fall. And . . . well, you know how I feel about your helping us out."

Miss Conrad caught a look in his eyes that brought the pink into her cheeks. "I'm only too glad to help. My sympathies are all with the Philistines, I'm afraid."

Hannahan's eyes said many things his lips were shy of putting into words, and then he remembered the need of haste. "Well, if I'm going to get the boys hazed into the camp of the Israelites by noon, I'll need to be moving. See yuh later, Miss Conrad."

Miss Conrad watched him out of sight, and there was a tender light in her eyes. When the dust had settled behind Chinto's flying heels, and the *cluckety-cluck* of them came so faint they could be heard only by the ear of faith, she turned and rode back around the rocky elbow of the hill, humming a little tune.

Beetle sat in a big cane-seated rocker and looked with the trustful gaze of a child into the magenta countenance of the Widow McCoy. He had pleased her mightily by his frank appreciation of her cookery, and by the sweet innocence of his expression.

"You're the picture of yer cousin, Jennie," she told him with some enthusiasm, and Beetle let his cupid-bow lips curve into a smile.

"Jennie's hair is darker than mine," he demurred, turning his eyes to the darkly red hair of Miss Conrad. Had Beetle been really as shy as he looked, he would have hesitated long before calling a strange young woman by her first name, even though it was all in the part he was playing.

"It's you have the true gold hair of a cherub," Mrs. McCoy declared. Jennie's cheeks went to red just then, and Hannahan, over on the stiff-backed sofa, gurgled and stored the remark away for future use.

"You must play for us, Eddie," put in Miss Conrad, laying spiteful emphasis upon the name, which made Beetle squirm inwardly. When she brought him Bud's guitar, he reproved her with lowered brows and passed it on to Parrot Tim. Miss Conrad had forgotten to inquire which instrument each man played.

"I'll try a whirl on your mandolin, if you've got it with you, Jen," Beetle said, and Miss Conrad hastened to bring it, remembering what Hannahan had told her about him.

Parrot Tim said never a word, as was his habit. But he tuned the guitar with nice precision, listened while Beetle picked a few tentative fragments of tunes, and nodded approval of the harmony. After that, there were no sounds but sweet ones. The Widow McCoy wore a fixed, ecstatic smile, and Bud himself, black browed and bullnecked, came and stood in the doorway, listening, with Patsy at his elbow.

"The foine music it is, then!" cried the widow breathlessly when they stopped.

"It makes me want to dance," Miss Conrad declared guilefully, and threw a sidelong smile at Bud and Patsy. "Play that waltz again, Eddie, there's a good little boy." She stood up and faced Bud McCoy, challenging him with her eyes.

Beetle swallowed his resentment at her tone, and swung again into the seductive measures of "Over the Waves". Bud, blinking in the unfamiliar sunshine of Miss Conrad's favor, went over and slipped an arm around her waist and waltzed clumsily until everything in the room—and there were many things—was kicked into an untidy little heap.

When Miss Conrad felt that the dance fever was rising in Bud's veins, she sat down, panting, beside Hannahan.

"I guess it's all over but the shouting," he managed to whisper when no one was looking, and Miss Conrad's long lashes drooped triumphant assent. She felt that she had done the thing rather cleverly, on the whole.

Bud's habitual frown relaxed under Miss Conrad's wistful smile. "We might have a little dance this evenin'. You ain't in no great rush, air yuh?" His eyes went to Hannahan in tacit recognition of his leadership.

Hannahan hesitated diplomatically over his cigarette papers. "We ought to hit the sod, and that's no dream," he parlayed, appearing to dally with temptation. "We didn't aim to do more than make a fashionable call on Jennie." His fingers twirled a paper into a tiny tube while his heart pounded at the sweetness of calling her that name.

"Sure, what's the odds? Ye've only the wance t'live, then," urged the widow. "We'd be proud t' have ye stop . . . an' it's a foine toime we c'n promise ye. An' Jennie does git that lonesome. . . ."

Hannahan showed deceitful signs of yielding, and looked doubtfully at his fellows. Beetle, answering that look, told him briefly that he was the doctor. Miss Conrad, leaning toward him in a way that set his blood more than ever a-jump, coaxed prettily so that his mind was almost tricked into the belief that he was being led into temptation, and not carrying out a prearranged plan. He promised to stay until midnight when, he said, they could make a night ride to Chinook, which was their destination. Hannahan liked to tell the truth whenever he could.

Miss Conrad straightway went off with the widow to help

make cakes and things, and Bud and Patsy caught up their horses and rode off to notify their neighbors. The "vanguard" sat out on the front steps and strummed melodious snatches for the delectation of the two in the kitchen, and smoked many cigarettes, and waited.

As the day grew weary and the sun slid away behind the hills, the wind grew weary, also, and rested. The night gave promise of dark stillness, with slow drifting clouds to mask the moon.

"Yuh want t' give it to 'em good and plenty," Beetle told Hannahan out in the corral when they went to feed their horses—and saddle them, also, in readiness for a quick get-away should circumstances render it necessary. Hannahan was going to "call" for the dancers.

"Yuh want," Beetle went on, "lots uh double-elbow and chassy-by-your-pardners, and swing on the corners. Make 'em hoe-'er-down-eight all yuh think they'll stand for. Sound'll travel like the devil tonight."

Hannahan's teeth showed white in the dusk. He reached out a gloved hand and patted Beetle's shoulder caressingly. "Right you are, Little Goldenhair," he murmured tenderly.

Beetle squirmed loose and swore vigorously. His face at that moment was not particularly cherubic. "Damn that old hen," he remarked, and stalked back to the house in a fit of ill temper that lasted all of five minutes.

At eight o'clock every man, woman, and child in the valley was waiting expectantly at the Widow McCoy's.

At nine o'clock, the big living room was filled to over-flowing with gyrating figures, and the overflow was footing it in the kitchen, with Hannahan standing in the connecting doorway, calling both ways at once. Beetle and Parrot Tim, their chairs perched upon a table pulled close to the doorway, looked down upon the dancers with faces calm, fingers flying, and hearts astir with the exhilarating sense of danger.

Far out on the bench land, a slow-moving blotch of shade swept steadily down to the valley's rim, with shadowy horsemen vaguely outlined here and there along the wavering border. The steaming breath from many wide-flaring nostrils rose mysteriously as a faint swishing crackle of dry buffalo grass mingled with the muffled thud of five thousand hoofs beating steadily on prairie sod.

At ten o'clock Beetle laid down his mandolin, fished a red-boxed harmonica from his coat pocket, handed it with a whisper to Hannahan, and stole out into the cool blackness to listen.

Hannahan had blown himself breathless before the mandolin shrilled again, high and sweet above the uproar. There was a pink splotch on Beetle's cheeks, and in his eyes the deep purple glow that came only under stress of a crisis. Parrot Tim recognized the signs and, leaning toward him, questioned with his calm gray eyes.

Beetle's dimpled chin lowered a scant half inch in answer. He turned to Hannahan. "Give 'em hell from now on," he urged under his breath. "Call a hot one, the hottest yuh know, and the longest."

Hannahan went out into the kitchen and poured near a quart of sweet spring water down his tired throat, and then went to work—the real work of the evening.

The Widow McCoy danced wisps of gray hair down into her eyes and seemed upon the verge of apoplexy, but Hannahan was merciless. Miss Conrad, flushed and disheveled, turned her eyes reproachfully his way, caught the meaning of his level brows and half-closed lids, and smiled encouragement instead of reproof as she whirled away like a leaf in the wind, in the endless chain—"Balance, swing!

Allemane left, chasse-by-your-pardner, balance, swing! Right hand to pardner and grand right-and-left with a double-elbow . . . balance, swing!"

The amount of swinging inflicted upon those trustful tillers of the Chiquita soil was amazing. It was a limp, exhausted company which made for the nearest seats when finally a string snapped and the mandolin stopped for repairs, and Hannahan hoarsely shouted the welcome command: "All promenade . . . you know where, and I don't care!"

But he did care. His heart misgave him as he leaned his long length, the picture of careless ease, against the door-jamb, shoved his hands deeply into his pockets, and watched Bud McCoy stumble out into the night.

Bud had been dancing with Miss Conrad, and his brain reeled with something more than the dizzying succession of swings. He could feel yet an electric thrill in his shoulder, where the gold-bronze head of Miss Conrad had rested for the fraction of a second during that last breathtaking whirl.

Beetle's head bent over the broken string; to all appearances, his mind was wholly absorbed in its mending.

Hannahan strolled over, and put his lips close to Beetle's ear. "Where was they when you was outside?" he whispered cautiously.

"Just coming into the field here. They ought t' be pretty well across by now. Can't yuh get busy with that mouth organ again? We got t' keep 'em inside."

"Bud McCoy's outside."

"The hell he is!" came from the lips of the cherub. He shifted uneasily in his chair. "Things'll begin t' tighten, then. He. . . ."

The voice of Bud McCoy bellowed through the room like a challenging bull: "Come on, boys! They's a herd at the ford!"

Instantly the room buzzed like a disturbed hive; like bees, men swarmed to the door, their haste retarding their exit. The shrewish tones of the Widow McCoy screamed angrily above the clamor.

The vanguard made for the kitchen, escaped by way of the back door, and raced away to the stables. After them came the Israelites, a cursing, vengeful mob headed by Bud and Patsy McCoy.

From out of the far darkness came the splash of water churned by many fording animals, and the indefinable murmur of the herd climbing the slope beyond. Once, the sharp tones of the foreman called out, and the words came clear cut through the black: "Rush 'em, boys . . . the grangers are coming!"

"If we could keep 'em here ten minutes . . . ," Hannahan groaned anxiously.

"I turned a trick that I guess'll hold 'em for a while," panted Beetle.

Bud McCoy made for the nearest horse, which happened to be Dave Hadley's, and seized the stirrup. Up he went, a black shape against the starlit sky—hovered for a breath—and came down bewildered. "What ails the damned saddle?" he demanded of no one in particular.

Nobody answered; other voices took up the question and repeated it in various forms. Horses began to circle and back away from their masters, snorting protest.

In the confusion, somebody broke into laughter—the rollicking, boyish laugh of mischief that recks not of consequences.

Bud wheeled upon the source. "Who was it switched all them saddles backward? Was it you, yuh damned gigglin' little doll-face?"

Beetle stopped laughing and straightened his slim height.

73

His fist plunked solidly as he smote the surprised leader of the Israelites.

"Hand it to 'im, Beetle!" Hannahan called from behind. "My money's on you!"

Patsy McCoy danced in the background and howled weird threats until Parrot Tim reached out a long, leisurely arm, caught him by the collar, and shook him violently. Then somebody detected Hannahan in the act of turning loose a horse, and after that the corral seemed filled mostly with arms, legs, and unseemly language.

A few there were who wisely refrained from active warfare and contented themselves with removing the saddles, which under Beetle's earlier manipulation pointed their horns rakishly to the rear, and readjusted them in the position nature and the manufacturers intended. Since, without exception, each horse developed an aggravated case of nerves, some time was consumed in the operation.

Parrot Tim wriggled himself free with the loss of his coat. He then felt under a squirming heap of humanity until he located what he shrewdly guessed was Beetle, who observed with much satisfaction that the heap did not seem to miss him, but continued to pummel one another indiscriminately and with much energy.

Two minutes after, the vanguard, battered but triumphant, splashed through the once more peaceful waters of the Chiquita, and halted on the farther shore to listen to the sounds of tumult in the corral of the Widow McCoy ere they galloped away.

"If old Jimmy Knauss don't give Jennie Conrad that little pinto pony to pay for this night, there'll be things doing," Hannahan remarked as they rode up the hill. "How do yuh stack up, Golden Hair?"

"Aw, shut up!" growled Beetle. "I bet Bud McCoy'll

count ten million before he says 'doll-face' t' me again, the way I punched his'n for him."

Parrot Tim rode for ten minutes with his chin drooped against his neck. Then he turned his head, looked back to where the Chiquita gleamed faintly under the stars, and spoke: "And the Philistines put themselves in array against Israel . . . and when they joined battle, Israel was smitten before the Philistines. . . . And the men of Israel rent their garments, and wept aloud that they were smitten!"

"They rent mine, too, if anybody should ask yuh," said Beetle.

The Deserter

Bud Cowan, top hand for the TL outfit back in Big Sandy, had told Bower of his narrow escape as a boy when Ute Indians attacked the Cowan Ranch during the 1879 Meeker Massacre in Wyoming. The family had accidentally left young Bud behind as they fled. He hid three long days in a cabin's shallow attic without food or water, before the Indians moved on. Bud's feat inspired part of this Flying U short story, which first appeared in *The Popular Magazine* (1/08). It points out the drawbacks of shooting first and asking questions later. Weary Davidson, Pink Perkins, and Happy Jack happily leave their dull line camp and head north. They stop overnight at a cabin near the Canadian border where mysterious noises disturb their sleep. By helping the fugitive they find in the attic, they unwittingly contribute to the tragic conclusion.

Jack Bates galloped up to the cabin at the head of One Man Coulée where Weary, Pink, and Happy Jack had been living the uneventful life of the line camp. He delivered a message that sent Pink's hat spinning up toward the blue—a message from Chip Bennett, foreman of the Flying U. It meant days in the saddle, hard gallops after horses rollicky from good grass and months of idleness; it meant living in the open next to the ground and to nature; it meant, in short, a return to that roving life of the range which the cowboy loves best of all.

The Flying U had bought a bunch of saddle horses up on the north fork of Milk River, which was Pink's old range.

Because he knew every foot of that country, Pink was chosen to go after them, with Weary and Happy Jack for help and companionship. They were to start at once, stop at the home ranch for a pack outfit and their string of horses, and the next morning would find them pushing toward the northern boundary of Uncle Sam's possessions.

The three hurriedly washed their dishes, swept the floor, and put the cabin to rights with a dispatch that spoke well for their domestic accomplishments, threw their personal belongings into war bags, rolled their beds, and caught up their horses. In half an hour they had climbed the ridge and headed blithely for Flying U Coulée, leaving the One Man line camp lying silent in the warm sunlight of early May.

The next sunrise found the little expedition on its way, alert, keen-eyed, glorying in freedom from the four-walled life. To look at them, you would have been slow to believe that they had spent weeks lying lazily upon their bunks, mourning because there were dishes to be washed, too lazy to decide whose duty it was to wash them, smoking cigarettes, and longing for spring.

That day and the next they traveled far, and the second night camped in a deserted cabin on a level stretch of grassland but a day's ride from the line. They were tired, and ate their supper almost silently. When dusk settled over the rangeland, they spread their blankets on the rough board floor, and lay down with little sighs of content at the long night of unbroken rest that would be theirs.

At midnight Weary, always a light sleeper, raised his head from the folded coat which served him for a pillow and listened. Clear white moonlight crept mysteriously through chinks in the cabin and made the shadows deep and black. Beyond the walls crickets were chirping breathlessly, and frogs *cr-ek, cr-ek, cr-eked* in tuneless medley along the marshy

water holes. Familiar sounds they were to Weary; he slapped viciously at an early mosquito that hummed monotonously in A-natural against his cheek, and lay down again, thinking he had dreamed it.

Two minutes later and he was on his elbow again. Nothing had changed—Pink and Happy Jack lay stretched beside him, breathing deep lungfuls of pure prairie air while they slept. Pink's face, as the moonlight lay softly upon it, was innocent and untroubled as the face of a baby. Weary looked down at him tenderly for a minute, and laid back quietly that he might not disturb him.

Then it came—the faint indefinable sound for which he was waiting. He listened, half tempted to believe that he imagined it all, only Weary was not the sort of man who imagines things at night.

In the white coolness outside, a horse sneezed the dew from his nostrils while he fed upon the crisp new grass, and the *crp-crp-crp* of his cropping cut sharply through the night murmurs. Weary's eyes swept the narrow confines of the cabin dubiously, unsatisfied. He rolled upon his side and readjusted his coat pillow impatiently. His brown head no more than touched it, than he was up again, listening.

Pink's ribs felt the nudge of Weary's elbow. Pink's long lashes lifted alertly before his lithe body moved a muscle— night guarding trains a man to silent awakenings.

"What the . . . ?" as memory came to him.

"Listen!"

Pink raised his head, and became motionless. After a minute or so his eyes sought Weary's in the moonlight. "What d'yuh reckon it is?" he whispered.

"Mama . . . you can search me," Weary whispered back.

"Can't be anybody in here," Pink argued under his breath. "Sounds outside, don't yuh think?"

For answer, Weary slipped into trousers and boots. He reached out and took his gun from its scabbard. Pink likewise clothed himself speedily, and got his fingers gripped on his gun.

Outside, the crickets shrilled more insistently, the nearest ones hushing precipitately at their approach. Together the two stole around the cabin, grimly expectant. The horses lifted their heads and eyed them questioningly, their hobbles clanking when they moved. Glory, staked out to an iron picket pin, walked as far as his rope would allow and nickered coaxingly, but Weary gave no heed. Watchfully the men circled the four walls and stopped at the door, baffled and bewildered.

"I guess we must be locoed, Weary," Pink remarked in an undertone. "There isn't anything."

"I heard it two or three times before I woke you," Weary contended. "It woke me up. I'll swear to the sound . . . but there sure isn't anyone out here."

They went in softly and looked keenly where the moonlight shone, and lighted a match to illuminate the dark corners. The floor was littered with their saddles, bridles, and pack outfits, for the evening had promised rain and their belongings had been stored inside. The blaze licked along the matchwood, flickered, and Pink dropped the charred remains to the floor.

"It's sure a puzzler, Cadwolloper," Weary remarked.

His voice was not yet silenced when he gripped Pink's shoulder. They stood like posts while a faint moan rose, lingered, and then died away.

"Aw, say!" The voice was Happy Jack's. "If yuh feel that bad, why don't yuh take a jolt uh Three H? They's a bottle somewheres in the outfit." He sat up, blinking sleepily at their shadowy forms.

"It ain't us," Pink told him shortly.

"Who is it, then?"

"Nobody. We've been out on a still hunt. There's nobody around the place but us."

They held their breaths while the sound wailed again in the gloom.

"I wonder if there's a cellar," Weary ventured.

"Naw," Pink answered. "I was by here when it was being built. It sets flat on the ground, and is banked with dirt besides. A mountain rat would have to dig. . . ."

Rising weirdly, faint yet unmistakable, they heard it again —a pitiful sound wrung from a man in misery.

"Is there a loft?" Weary looked speculatively at the ceiling. "If there is, it must be up there, seeing it ain't anywhere else."

Pink struck another match that burned slowly while the uncanny moan rose and silenced speech. The three craned their necks while they listened. Pink picked his way carefully through the litter on the floor, searching the gloom above.

"Over here's a manhole," he announced softly, "but the trap is closed. Give me a shoulder, one of yuh . . . I'm going up."

"And get the top of your head shot off," Weary prophesied. "You keep down from there . . . I'm going up there myself."

But Pink had his own opinion of that. He went up Weary's shoulder like a cat, and pushed at the trap cautiously.

"Cadwolloper, you little devil, you'll be killed," Weary told him anxiously while he stood motionless that Pink might not fall.

"Hand me some matches and close your face," Pink leaned to whisper.

A tiny flame glowed in the blackness above, and the two below held their breaths and kept their guns ready for use.

Pink drew carefully through the opening, and recklessly struck another match. He was head and shoulders in the loft, and his heels were pressing hard on Weary's shoulders. Happy Jack thoughtfully moved close, and took a foot to divide the burden, and Weary thanked him with a glance.

Looking up, they could see Pink level his gun at something. "Here, yuh come out uh that," he commanded as harshly as was possible for his vocal chords.

Came a confused, scuffling sound as of booted feet drawn hastily across the flimsy boards.

"Go easy there with that gun, stranger," came a voice. "I'll be good."

"You'd better," Pink growled somewhere in his throat.

Then his match went out and blotted the scene, and the two below breathed hard with fear for him. They could not help, for the manhole would not admit more than one at a time. But Pink was undismayed although he knew the situation to be ticklish. His voice rose menacingly in the blackness of the loft.

"Don't yuh move an eye-winker, darn yuh. I'm the wildcat uh the cow country. I can see in the dark. I was born in a mess wagon, cradled in a sourdough keg. My gait is the lightning," he chanted chestily, "and hell is in my breath. Peace troubles my mind, I love the sight uh blood, and the groans uh dying men is music to my ears!"

By then Pink had crawled warily into the loft with the unknown. "Now, yuh skulking varmint, if yuh value your worthless carcass, take a sneak down that hole into the arms uh my gang. And don't yuh move a muscle, or I'll shoot to kill."

As the somewhat contradictory command rolled sonorously forth, a man breathed audibly in the black shadows of the corner. Pink produced another match, thereby giving the lie to his cat-like sight. "Are yuh going?" he thundered. "Or are yuh waiting to be took to pieces and handed down in fragments?"

"I'm studying out how I can go without moving a muscle. It's sure puzzling me, stranger."

"Yuh better go first, and do your studying afterward. I'll count three and. . . ."

"You're the doctor."

Straightway a pair of long legs dangled through the opening, and were seized eagerly by Weary and Happy Jack. Up in the loft, the owner of the legs clutched involuntarily at the rough boards to save himself, but four strong hands are long odds against two, and the body speedily followed the legs into the vaguely moonlit room.

Pink, grinning and triumphant, dropped lightly down beside him. He did not look the fearsome being he had proclaimed himself even in that half light, and the captive eyed him agape, taking in every detail of his figure from tousled yellow curls, round cherubic face, and long-lashed beautiful eyes, to boots run over at the heels and showing shiny where the spurs had rubbed. Pink stared unwinkingly back.

"So you're the wildcat uh the cow country?" drawled the captive. "Your gait is the lightning and hell is in your breath, huh? Well now, young 'un, that's a mighty pretty little piece, and yuh said it real good . . . but, if I was you, I wouldn't go shouting it promiscuous around strangers. They're liable to take yuh serious and cut loose on yuh with a gun. All that saved yuh tonight is I don't happen to have one. About how often do yuh take them spells?"

Pink's glance never wavered, although he did not relish being addressed as "young 'un"—he who was past twenty-two years old. "Every now and then," he retorted mildly. "And when I do, I notice folks generally promise to be good."

"They do," assented the other, "especially when they're woke up sudden in the dark, and can't see but what it's a real man broke loose and hunting trouble. Got a cigarette paper handy?"

"Sure." Pink proffered the materials for a smoke. "Maybe yuh don't mind explaining how yuh come to pick on the loft of an old shack to sleep in, when there's lots uh room and good company down below."

The stranger calmly rolled a cigarette, handed papers and tobacco back to Pink, and accepted a match from Weary.

"Seeing you're 'punchers, I'll chance your being able to savvy the tale uh woe I'm about to tell. The play come up this way . . . I was punching cows down Miles City way, and had throwed in with a mighty nice boy that had a temper . . . likewise a reputation for burning powder, reckless and free. No need going into details. But a little while back, him and I was riding the range together, when we bumps into a jasper that this friend uh mine didn't love none to speak of. They mixed right there, and, when the smoke clears, my friend's gun is oozing powder smoke, and the other fellow is likewise oozing blood through a hole in his head. He's all in, and we drift.

"Now, they's no evidence against my friend, but me. He's got the rep, however, and they gather him in on suspicion. Likewise they take me in for a witness. But when it comes to bucking these gay lawyer sharps, and telling a good, truthful-looking lie and sticking to it, I don't feel I'm there with the goods. Also, I'd swear my mother was a man, before I'd send my friend up to be star guest at a necktie party . . . which would sure be the case, as the man he smoked up has got folks with dough and a plenty revengeful nature.

"So, being I get a chance to sneak, I do so. And that's how comes it I'm numbered among the missing. I'm headed for Canada, if anybody should ask yuh. And my horse played out on me, day before yesterday, and sent me afoot. Likewise, when I gathered in a stray and stepped up on him to continue my travels, he pawed several stars out uh the sky, rooted up several acres uh sod with his nose, and decamps plumb out uh the country with my saddle. And in the mix-up I lost my gun and couldn't find it again.

"So, when you fellows hove in sight last night, I didn't know who yuh was or what was your business . . . and not having a strong desire to mix in society, I made myself invisible. And I'd be plumb tickled to know how yuh got next to me."

The three looked at one another.

"Yuh took to groaning," Weary explained, "and woke me up. Uh course, I was bound to investigate those strange sounds."

"Well, I went to sleep," the stranger explained apologetically. "A game leg and an empty stomach is mighty liable to start a fellow out with some sounds, when he's asleep and don't know it. I'm sure sorry I disturbed your slumbers, and, if you'll excuse me, I'll go back and try to behave better."

Pink walked to the door, opened it, and went out into the moonlight. Presently he poked his head in and asked Happy Jack where the dickens he'd put the coffee pot. A fire was crackling outside and throwing wavering, ruddy beams in through the door. Happy Jack grunted, got up, and found the coffee pot, and Pink disappeared. Soon the air hung heavy with savory smells, and a few minutes later the stranger was eating hungrily, and assuring the three that they were sure all right, and the real article.

Pink went out again, and Weary, catching his eye, followed. Then Happy Jack joined them, and they drew off a few paces and consulted in low tones.

"We've got to help him out," Pink began, with characteristic decision.

"Yes, and git pinched ourselves for it," put in Happy Jack pessimistically.

"No, we won't. Who's to know? And so help me, Josephine, he strikes me as the whitest fellow I've met! I'd 'a' hit the trail anytime I had to help a friend or else perjure myself. And so would you. He's dead safe over the line. They can't bring a man back from there to give evidence . . . not even in a murder case. We've just got to help him."

"I'm sure willing, Cadwolloper, but we're helpless. We can stake him to grub, but that won't help him much . . . not if they're after him. It's a long walk from here to the line." Weary looked meditatively away to the dim northern skyline.

"Well," Pink spoke with some hesitation, "I guess he can ride Toots. He's my own private horse, and he won't be missed. And if one of you fellows'll lend him a gun, he ought to make out all right."

"Aw, say!" began Happy Jack dissentingly, but Pink turned on him fiercely. "What if it was you?" he demanded. "Wouldn't you look to any cowpunchers yuh met to help yuh out uh the scrape? And wouldn't they do it? What kind of a man are yuh, anyway?"

"Aw, g'wan! He . . . he can have my gun, if that'll do him any good."

"I've got an extra coat in my war bag," said Weary promptly. "I took notice he didn't have any on, and so I make a guess it was tied behind his saddle when the big set-to come off with the strange horse, and he lost it. We'll have to get busy or he won't get far before daybreak. Yuh can't rightly call Toots a drifter . . . his legs is too short."

"Yuh needn't worry about Toots's legs," reproved Pink with dignity. "If he ain't a drifter, he's a stayer. He can put his

85

nibs across the line about as quick as your wonderful Glory . . . if anybody should ask yuh."

Weary laughed good-humoredly, and they returned to the cabin and told the stranger what they were going to do for him, and the stranger put out his hand and said they were the whitest bunch he'd met in many a day, and he was sure obliged to them, and if they ever got in a tight place, and he was anywhere near, to just let him know.

"You'll have to ride with a blanket," apologized Pink, all aglow with their generous deed. "You can leave the horse at Beecher's . . . first ranch yuh strike on Ten Mile, just over the line. And I'll give yuh a note to Rowdy Vaughan, a friend uh mine that's running an outfit farther north, on the Red Deer. He'll give yuh work, if yuh want it."

They went to work with much haste, giving directions and advice while they made ready. In fifteen minutes they stood outside the cabin and watched the fugitive ride swiftly away in the moonlight with Happy Jack's much-prized gun strapped around his middle, with Weary's coat buttoned close around him, and with Pink's beloved Toots galloping steadily between his knees. They stood until his outline blurred, grew indistinct, then faded utterly while the faint beat of Toot's galloping hoofs died to silence and the frogs, startled to momentary silence as they passed, took up again their reedy song where they had left off and *cr-ek, cr-eked* gratingly in the dim, lonely hollows. The crickets took to chirping indefatigably again, and the horses went back to cropping the sweet, dewy grasses.

The three turned and went in, and meditatively pulled off their boots.

"Anyway," said Weary, with a faint sigh, "we've got the poor devil off our minds . . . and I sure hope he gets through all right."

"Aw, g'wan!" snarled Happy Jack. "We're jest beginning t' git him *on* our minds. I betcha Pink never sees his horse again . . . nor me my gun. I betcha he was jest stringing us. I betcha. . . ."

"You shut up," snapped Pink. "Would you rather 'a' handed him over to whoever's after him, or left him to starve? What ails yuh, anyhow?"

Happy Jack did not answer the questions. They lay listening to the familiar night noises, and their thoughts followed the fugitive in his flight to the north where lay safety. Not one of them could inwardly regret the help they had given him, a fellow cow-puncher in trouble.

Pink came in from looking after the horses, and his eyes were a deeper blue than usual. "There's four or five riders headed straight for this shack, boys. I guess they're after him, all right. We don't know anything, uh course, and, for heaven's sake, Happy, either get that look uh guilt off your face, or else go crawl into the loft. One look at you'll give the whole deal away."

He picked up a basin and began industriously mixing some baking powder flapjacks. He looked exceedingly innocent and at peace with the world and himself—not in the least like Happy Jack, who fidgeted in and out of the door like a materialized guilty conscience.

The riders galloped up and stopped just short of the little campfire where the coffee was steaming aromatically.

"Hello," greeted Weary cheerfully. "Just in time for breakfast."

"We've had ours," said one, glancing about him watchfully. "We camped down below here a couple uh miles."

"Then you're sure early risers," commented Weary placidly, and adjusted an ember more to his liking.

"Seen anything of a man . . . a soldier, he is . . . around

here?" asked one, who gave unmistakable evidence of being a soldier and an officer.

Weary shook his head vaguely in reply.

Pink came to the door with his basin of batter and a frying pan, and greeted them with a nod. "What's that about soldiers?" he inquired mildly.

"They want to know if we've seen a soldier running around loose," Weary explained sweetly. "Soldiers must be getting scarce, to hotfoot over the country after one lone one, don't yuh think?"

"He ain't just a plain deserter," said the officer grimly. "He's worse'n that. He rolled a man in Havre, got off with everything from the poor devil . . . even to a letter from his best girl . . . and pulled his freight, the low-down skunk. He's afoot, and we've reason to think he has got into civilian clothes. He wasn't satisfied with robbing the fellow . . . had to stick a knife into him besides."

"He must sure be a peach," observed Pink, not daring to look toward Happy Jack, who was contorting his face agonizingly just inside the door. "What sort of looking fellow was he? We're going on up to the line after horses . . . and it may be our luck to run onto him."

"Well," said the officer, "he's tall and well-built, and has the look of a cowpuncher . . . used to be one, before he enlisted. And he's got a smooth tongue, and will probably tell you a tale that don't jibe with the truth none too well. If you meet him, boys, I wish you'd take him in, and let us know. We'll make it right with you."

He gave further unsavory details of the fellow's record, and they rode off. The three gazed after them soberly.

"What'd I *tell* yuh?" began Happy Jack, querulously triumphant. "I know'd all the time the fellow was stringing us. Pink's so darn' charitable . . . he couldn't see how coarse the

story was. Oh, no! He had t' go and stake him to Toots and
my gun. . . ."

"Yuh offered the gun yourself," Pink reminded indignantly.

"Aw, g'wan! Didn't I tell yuh not t' be so blame generous?
But, oh, no! It was . . . 'what if *you* was in his place?' . . . and
all that. It was either give up my gun or have you fellows both
throwing it into me about being mean and stingy and not
helping the poor devil out. I guess next time yuh won't be so
darn' easy. I *told* yuh yuh'd never see your little old duck-leg
Toots again. . . ."

That was too much. Pink dropped the frying pan and went
at him viciously. They rolled in the grass and pummeled each
other with much venom and in silence, till Weary interfered
and pulled Pink off—Pink usually was on top, in a mix-up of
that sort—and pacified them as best he could.

"The thing for us to do is quit bellyaching and go overhaul
our friend. He's welcome to Happy's gun, but blamed if he's
going to get off with my coat!"

Happy Jack scowled at the two, and retreated sullenly
inside. "Aw, you two smart boys . . . yuh make me tired. He
did work yuh both to a finish, and you know it. And yuh mark
my words . . . you won't overhaul him, and yuh won't ever see
your stuff ag'in. He's likely laughing up his sleeve right now,
t' think how easy he worked yuh."

"Oh, shut up!" cried Pink sharply.

"I tell yuh what," soothed Weary, going back to the interrupted breakfast, "Happy's so gay, we'll just let him go on
with the horses and outfit, while we ride ahead and see if we
can't come up with the fellow. And seeing Happy don't
expect his gun back, we'll let his nibs keep it."

"G'wan! Good reason why . . . yuh won't git a chanst t' git
it back."

"What'll yuh bet?" Weary placidly poured himself a cup of coffee.

"I'll bet yuh the gun. If yuh git it . . . which yuh won't . . . it's yours, belt and all. I paid twenty dollars for that gun." Happy sighed lugubriously.

"Then it's *my* gun, and I'll be wearing it before night. Mama, I wish you fellows would come and eat. Time's worth a heap to us, right now."

They ate to the tune of Happy's grumbling. Twice Weary held Pink back when he would fain have fought again, so that it was not a cheerful meal, nor were there any of the laughs that help digestion. Then Weary and Pink saddled their fleetest mounts, left Happy Jack with explicit directions just where to meet them that night, and galloped away to the north—their horses kicking up sweet morning smells from the young grass, their spurs jingling rhythmically to the motion of their swinging heels.

Long miles they rode, and stopped at noon for a bite to eat and to rest their horses. Then they tightened cinches and went on, always to the north, where stretched the boundary between our country and the King's. The sun struck hotly from the west when they topped a knoll and saw a scene that brought them up short.

Below, in a brushy creek bottom, grazed Toots with hanging bridle reins. Off to one side, from a clump of close-huddled willows, a little blue smoke puff curled lazily. Nearer, from the rock-strewn hillside just beneath, four rifles barked vicious reply.

The two looked at each other with unsmiling eyes.

"If we had Toots back safe, I'd wish the poor devil could get off clear," said Pink gravely. "It ain't far to the line, from here."

"He can't, though. Happy's gun is pickings for four rifles

like they're handling. It'll be all day for him."

Five minutes, then ten, they sat on the hilltop and watched the pitifully uneven battle below. Toots raised his head, looked up at the curling smoke puffs, and wisely moved farther down to the creek out of range, then he went back to his feeding. From the willow clump came spiteful little cracks from the revolver, but the range was hopelessly long. It was simply dogged persistence that kept the fellow shooting.

"I wonder how many shells Happy had in his belt?" Weary remarked in an undertone.

Pink shook his head. His lips were shut tightly, and his eyes were a deep purple. "It's a damn' shame. I don't care if he did play us for suckers. For half a cent I'd take a hand in this myself. Four against one . . . oh, hell!"

Weary's eyes blurred while he shook his head. "I guess he's got it coming . . . but it does look like plumb murder. I wish to. . . ."

The four rifles zipped bullets into the willow clump. There was no dogged revolver shot in answer.

Pink groaned. "I guess the shells are all gone," he said huskily. "It's a damn', dirty shame!"

"It sure is."

They waited, as did the four on the hillside below. Another volley they sent, and still the willow clump gave no sign. The four consulted, and moved cautiously closer.

"I'm going down!" Pink cried defiantly. "I'll tell those butchers how a white man looks at such things, if it's the last thing I do on earth."

Weary descended with him, both vindictively swearing threats against the officer and his men. The four below had reached the willow clump, sent four more bullets tentatively into its shadiest nooks, and, still getting no sign, walked boldly up to the place. They parted the bushes, looked in, and drew back hastily. Even at a distance, the two could see how gray were the men's faces.

"They ought to feel real good . . . I guess they got him," gritted Pink. Then they themselves came up to the place.

"Oh, it's you," greeted the officer dully. "I hope you boys can keep quiet about this . . . though it isn't our fault. We ordered this man to surrender, and he began to fight. It's his own fault . . . only . . . the trouble is . . . it's not the man we wanted!"

Pink and Weary sat stunned in their saddles.

"I know him," spoke up one of the men in a hushed tone. "He's a cowpuncher that used to be down Miles City way . . . and a damn' nice boy. I don't know what he's doing here, though."

"Just making a mark for you"—never mind what—"butchers to shoot at for practice. You're a brave lot, ain't yuh? Four against one . . . and him the wrong one! Oh, hell!"

Pink would have said more—he would have cursed them till they shriveled before him—but his voice broke utterly. He could not, even by setting his teeth hard, hold steady his quivering chin. He got down with his back to the others that they might not see how utterly his control was broken, knelt beside the long, lifeless figure, and placed the hat tenderly over the unseeing eyes. Then he unbuckled Happy Jack's gun belt, and rose shakily.

"He was whiter than any of you butchers'll ever be," he said. "He was going north, and we helped him out last night, with the horse and gun. And I hope to God you'll see his face every night of your lives, you murderers. Come on, Happy Jack, I guess this is your gun. I'll round up Toots, and we'll go."

"I hope," began the officer placatingly, "you understand. . . ."

"Oh, shut up! For half a cent, I'd take a shot at yuh," Pink snarled from the saddle, where he had swung after giving up the gun to Happy Jack.

They rode slowly down to where Toots stood eying them with low, nickering welcome, and not once did they look back.

The Terror

B. M. Bower got a letter in 1906 from a young girl who wanted to know what it would cost to travel West and become a cowboy. As many adolescents do, the girl took seriously everything she read about the subject—even nonsense like the story Bower criticized in "The Western Tone", another story in this book. The naïve youngster in "The Terror", a lively tale first published in *The Popular Magazine* (12/1/09), is even more determined to live out his wild fantasies. Hungry and broke in northern Montana, he encounters a bachelor rancher who takes him in and soon regrets his generosity. Then the rancher discovers a secret that leads to a surprising solution, but, as in many Bower stories, a happy ending is only suggested.

With the yellow sandstone ledge at his back and cat tongues of flame licking daintily the dry twigs he had gathered, Cliff Wayne settled down upon his boot heels and was at peace with his world. With all of it, save Rocket—and he was so accustomed to being at war with that particular cayuse that his resentment was a familiar mood, rather than an active, absorbing passion. When one has experienced nearly every discomfort that the inventions of a mouse-colored horse may inflict, being left afoot on the prairie fifteen miles from home loses the semblance of a tragedy and becomes merely an unpleasant incident.

Cliff whittled a cottonwood stick to a sharp point, impaled the hindquarters of a rabbit he had shot, and held the pink flesh to the fire. He had no salt, but he was not worrying much over that. It would not be the first time that his supper had wanted its savor. Neither would it be his first night beside a campfire with no bed to ease his bones upon. These also were merely unpleasant incidents, such as may come at any time to a man. The affair lacked even the keen edge of novelty, and it never occurred to Cliff that it might be regarded by some as an adventure.

It took the unmistakable sound of a shod hoof striking sharply against a rock to bring into his eyes more than a brooding meditation, and to make him peer curiously into the night.

"Can't be that fool Rocket . . . he's home, long ago. Trust *him!*" He listened, glanced uncertainly at the roasting rabbit hams, laid them down upon a fairly clean rock that was near, and stood up. He listened again. It seemed to him that he heard cautious footsteps moving out there where the dark hung like a straight black curtain, and he could not see beyond.

"Hello!" he called out tentatively, still not sure of the sound.

"A . . . a . . . throw up your hands! Not a move or . . . or I fire . . . or you're a dead man!"

It startled Cliff—that voice shrilling at him from the mysterious dark. "What the mischief . . . ?" he began amazedly.

"One false move and . . . and you drop like a log!" threatened the voice. It was a very young voice—and it was a very frightened voice, for all its shrill, bloodthirsty utterances.

Cliff laughed a bit. "You're it!" he called, and thrust his hands ostentatiously toward the dim star sprinkle. "They're up . . . come and get me."

He heard stumbling steps, the rattle of a stone or two, the *click* of hoofs. Presently he could see a round, big-eyed face

staring out of the dark, with the vague shape of a horse behind
—and then they stood out clearly in the firelight.

Cliff laughed again. "Are you the new sheriff, mistaking
me for a sure-enough outlaw, or are yuh the latest thing in
badmen yourself?" he inquired, taking down his hands
unconsciously, because it was uncomfortable holding them
up in the air.

"I ain't either one," retorted the newcomer defensively. "I
just wanted to git the drop before you got it. You can take
your hands down," he permitted rather tardily, "but, take
warning, I won't stand for any funny business. I've got a
gun."

"I can see yuh have. I was wondering if you was packing it,
or if it was packing you. Ain't yuh out kinda late for a kid?
Your mamma might be worrying about yuh."

"Aw, cut it ou-u-t!" Probably a million boys of twelve, or
thereabouts, have commanded the same thing, in exactly the
same tone. The tone was of the town and seemed out of
keeping here in the dark solitude, with only the stars to show
where was the sky. "I'm runnin' my own show. Say, who are
you, mister?"

"Have a seat," invited Cliff, taking up the rabbit hams
again and inspecting them critically. "Wayne's my name. Are
yuh hungry? There ain't any ranch close around here . . . yuh
must have come a long ways. Are you lost?"

"No," said the boy, still on his guard. "I ain't lost. And
yuh better not ask too many questions, either. Out West
here," he added darkly, "it ain't safe."

"Oh . . . ain't it?" Cliff leaned solicitously over the roasting
flesh.

"Uh course," began the boy after a minute or two of
silence, "I don't mind telling yuh that I've run away from
home. I won't tell yuh where it is, or . . . or my name. I'm

going to see the world, and be a cowboy, and ride wild bronchos, and . . . and fight Injuns. Maybe I'll be a stage robber, if the world turns ag'inst me and I'm drove to it.

"Yuh needn't be afraid, though," he added, after another minute of disconcerting silence. "I like your looks, and I'll act on the square with you . . . unless yuh play me false. Then . . . beware!"

Cliff, under the shadow of his hat brim, eyed the boy long. He had come from a town himself, and not so long ago that he had forgotten some of the types it breeds. "I'll gamble you was a messenger kid before yuh hit the trail," he hazarded involuntarily.

"What's it to yuh?" retorted the boy.

"It ain't anything. Only, yuh had too much time to read . . . it must 'a' been a small burg yuh hailed from . . . and yuh read the wrong brand uh stuff. Yuh better toddle back home, sonny. The Indians has all been killed off, and the bronc's have all been rode to death, and the cows have all been punched up the last chute into kingdom come. You're too late for the circus, kid . . . and that's a fact. Have some rabbit? It's fine if you're hungry enough."

The boy accepted a leg, but he was plainly displeased. "Say, I'm giving it to yuh straight! Yuh needn't feed me any uh that run-back-to-your-maw dope," he said, setting his teeth into the juiciest part of the meat. "I've heard it all the way out here. I started on my wheel, and made thirty-five miles a day on an average . . . till the roads got too rough . . . and every stopping place somebody'd hand me a bunch uh Sunday-school dope about my broken-hearted mother, and so on. Now you cut it out before yuh begin, see? My old man croaked years back, and my mother's married and ain't hurting none over me. She's glad I pulled out, I bet. Me and this new mark didn't hit it off a little bit. I ain't goin' back.

I'm out West, and I'm goin' to stay. See? And lemme give yuh a tip. Don't yuh call me sonny. I'm fifteen, and I can put a bullet through a man as far as I can see him . . . and I would, too, if he give me just cause! I ain't homesick, and I ain't going to be. I. . . ."

"You're a holy terror, ain't yuh?" Cliff put in admiringly, looking up over the clean-picked bone he held.

"That's what I am, all right," agreed the boy proudly. "And if you'll call me that for my name, I'll stand by you when the whole world is ag'inst yuh."

He was a queer mixture of innocence, city toughness, and the shoddy heroics which cheap novels and third-rate theaters breed. Cliff, studying him sidelong while he set the front legs of the rabbit to roasting, gave over the vague intention he had formed of questioning the wisdom of this flight into the wilderness.

"You're all right, old-timer," he said cheerfully. "I didn't mean to show any bad manners, or hand out advice to a man that's able to take care of himself. I've kinda been there myself. I pulled out kinda sudden and unexpected from a town . . . well, a good long walk from here. I don't know as I was quite as young as you, but I was plumb ignorant of the game I was going up against, and. . . ."

"Did you want to scalp Indians?"

"Well . . ."—Cliff gave a twitch to his hat, that it might shield his face from the glare of the flame that wrapped a dry stick he had just put on—"my temper was some bloodthirsty, all right. But I never scalped anything but wolves and coyotes . . . and I never held up any stage."

"What *did* you do?" The boy plainly demanded tumultuous history. "Anyway," he sighed contentedly, "yuh didn't run back to your maw."

"I didn't have any to run back to," said Cliff, and tested

the rabbit legs very carefully. "I got into about as many scrapes as Buckskin Ned. . . ."

"Go awn and tell about 'em."

Cliff shook his head vaguely.

"Did yuh ever kill a man, mister?"

Cliff offered the boy a rabbit leg before he answered. "Remember what yuh told me about it not being safe to ask too many questions?" he parried gruffly. "I might turn around and ask yuh where yuh got that cayuse, out there. I don't reckon yuh picked him off a sagebrush."

"I sold my wheel for twenty-five dollars when the roads got too poor to make any time on. It was a peach, and it cost sixty-five dollars new . . . my stepdad give it to me for a wedding present, when he married Maw . . . and I only used it about six months, so it was good as new. I never had but two punctures and a blow-out the whole time, and had to get the front wheel trued up, and a spoke or two put in the hind wheel where I run into a bunch uh bailing wire in an alley one night. I had a three-dollar-and-a-half lamp, and a full set uh tools, and a dollar pump, and a new bell that was worth six bits, and new mudguards. Why, it was like finding money to the guy that got it for twenty-five! So then I beat it out uh that town on a freight, and rode as far as I could . . . till they got after me and was going to send me back. So I bought that old skate out there, and that saddle, for twenty-five dollars, and pulled out into the country."

"And the gun?" queried Cliff politely.

"Aw . . . the gun is one I traded my solid gold cuff buttons and a Kodak for. I got it from the same fellow that sold me the horse."

"All right, we'll let it go at that." Cliff permitted his brows to relax. "If yuh want to bunk with me, you'd better crawl over here next the bank. The sand's softer than that rock.

How far did yuh come today?"

"I dunno. I did an awful lot of riding, but I don't believe I covered many miles . . . with that!" He jerked his hand contemptuously toward the horse, dimly outlined in that vague light where the fire glow fell short and the outer dark crept close. "What about him? Hadn't he ought to be unsaddled, or . . . something?"

"I'll look after the hoss. You bog down there and go to sleep."

When Cliff came back, the boy lay asleep, curled like a puppy between the fire and the bank. Cliff stood a minute, looking down at him. "Wouldn't it jar yuh . . . a kid the size uh that one!" He stooped and spread over him the saddle blanket he had brought from the horse. "A kid the size uh that one," he repeated musingly, and sat down with his knees drawn up and his hands clasped loosely around them, staring moodily into the fire.

The night grew old. The Big Dipper swung slowly around in the blue-black sky, keeping two twinkly eyes always vigilantly turned upon the North Star. Later a warped, languid moon rose and waded heavily through a rift of clouds, turning the velvety black of the night into a murky half light. The horse sneezed over the grass he was nosing out among the rocks, and, when he had filled to his satisfaction, lay down, a black lump of shade near the dully glowing fire.

Still Cliff sat hunched together near the boy, and moved only when the fire needed replenishing, or when the child, restless in his sleep, threw off the saddle blanket from his shoulders and Cliff reached out to tuck it snugly about him.

When the east began to lighten and turn pink, he arose, tucked the saddle blanket closer, and went quietly away down the coulée. Two rabbits he might have got before he took his gun from his hip, but he did not wish to awaken the boy by shooting so close to where he slept. He was gone an hour, and came back with two rabbits skinned and washed clean down by the spring that had a brackish taste of mineral, before the child sat up, bewildered.

"What do yuh say," Cliff began, awkwardly simulating carelessness, "to stopping with me for a spell? I've got a little ranch uh my own over here in the foothills, and I do need a man sometimes . . . for company. You know how it is when a fellow lives alone a while . . . he wants somebody to talk to."

The boy eyed him with some suspicion and more relief. "If you ain't just kidding me so yuh can send me back home"— he hesitated—"I'll go and live with yuh. Will yuh tell me your adventures with Injuns and . . . and robbers and bears?"

"I reckon," Cliff promised rashly.

That is how the element of discomfort came into the life of Cliff Wayne, small rancher and sometime cowboy. By daylight, the boy had shown certain attractive features, such as big, round, blue eyes, and hair that curled in little soft rings around his forehead. His vocabulary was startling at times, and his ambitions were not altogether laudable, but about him clung an elusive atmosphere that stirred to life the memory of something sweet, something bitter, something lost in the past years. Cliff felt it vaguely at times, keenly at others. It urged him toward the immediate protection of the lad.

It seemed a simple matter to take charge of a runaway boy of twelve—the extra three years he had claimed were afterward confessed to be a lie—until such time as his people might be located and notified of his whereabouts and his safety. Cliff felt very optimistic, right at the beginning. The boy would unguardedly name his town or his county—his state, surely!—and thereby give the necessary clue, or he would grow dissatisfied and homesick when he found how little this West resembled the West of the stories he had absorbed so greedily. And then Cliff would notify his mother and send him back, and incidentally feel that deep satisfaction which comes of doing a good deed well.

In reality, The Terror—he clung tenaciously to the name, and would own no other—manifested a desire to do things that were impracticable—immoral, even—from Cliff Wayne's tolerant viewpoint. He lived entirely in the present and the future, refusing to become homesick or to mention anything that lay behind that spectacular arrival at the campfire. He demanded that there be Indians to lie in ambush and rise inopportunely with blood-curdling yells. He wanted Cliff's cattle—a couple of hundred, range herded on the wide bottoms—to stampede over a precipice. Once he came near doing it—except that the precipice was merely a ten-foot washout, and Cliff discovered him in time to prevent disaster. Also, he formed the uncomfortable habit of assuming that every chance visitor was a train robber and a fugitive, and once interrupted an absorbing hand of pinochle which Cliff was playing with a half-breed caller, by bursting into the shack crying: "Fly for your life! A posse is galloping into view up the coulée!"

It happened that the half-breed owned a conscience not quite clear because of a certain little business of revised brands. He flew, and that pleased The Terror immensely— until the 'breed, reconnoitering from the rocks at the top of the coulée wall, recognized the lie, and came back shouting threats. Then it was The Terror that flew, and remained in hiding for the rest of that day.

Such things may or may not be amusing, just at first; certainly they pall quickly, even when mitigated by an elusively attractive personality. In a month Cliff looked upon The Terror as quite meriting the name and felt that his permanent absence would be extremely desirable. He did not even care so much whether the boy went home or strayed farther afield —so long as he left him, Cliff Wayne, in peace.

He made one concession to his conscience. He rode, after much meditation, to the nearest town where was a newspaper and advertised the runaway much as he would a stray horse. But nothing came of it, except the extreme displeasure of The Terror when he chanced two weeks later upon the item.

"Anyway, it won't do yuh no good, Mister Smarty," he finished, after a season of startling recrimination. "Back where I come from, they never even heard the name of the town where this vile sheet is printed. They won't see this in a thousand years. But I'll keep this, and some distant future day I'll get even with you. You're a traitor. Daniel Boone had a traitor friend, and he got even, you bet!" He unpinned a certain rent in the lining of his Norfolk jacket, and took from within a small flat package.

"Daniel Boone carried the picture of his little sister and a lock of her hair in the lining of his coat," he confided, forgetting his anger. "When the stars came out in the sky, and the wind moaned like a lost soul in the feathery tops of the pines, he would look at the picture and talk about things. And once they saved his life when the Indians got him, and they thought it was Great Spirit medicine. They were going to torture him, but they fell on their faces and made him chief."

"Uhn-huh." Cliff rolled a cigarette, and eyed the package askance. "Is that your . . . ?"

"It's just a stamp picture, and she ain't little like Daniel Boone's, with the face of an angel and golden curls. Hers is red, and she's big and old. But I ain't got any other sister, so I had to make it do." He sighed, and unwrapped several feet of string.

"Let's see it," said Cliff, his eyes showing interest.

B. M. Bower

"Aw, she ain't anything like Daniel Boone's sister . . . and she was awful mad when I chopped off that lock uh hair. I took it out uh her pompadour, and she had to do her hair another way so it wouldn't show."

Cliff, the cigarette untwisted and unlighted in his fingers, was staring down at the picture and at the long, silky lock of hair that was not so much red as a coppery brown. He did not appear to be listening. When The Terror took it back from his clasp, he drew a deep breath and stared queerly at the boy.

"About how old did you say she is?" he asked, fumbling for a match. "Twenty-four or five, maybe?"

The Terror eyed him suspiciously. "I never said. I said she was growed up. And she ain't the only big growed-up girl with red hair, Mister Smarty. Yuh can't catch me up on that. Yuh can't catch me at all . . . yuh ain't smooth enough!" He grinned, and folded the clipping away with the picture, winding it carefully with the string and tying the package securely. He put it back inside the lining of his coat and pinned the rent together.

"I want some shells," he announced with the imperious tone of unfearing childhood. "I'm going up the coulée. Maybe there's some Indians in ambush up there, today. I heard war whoops in the night, and an owl hooted three times in the rocks up there. Pretty soon a coyote howled over there" —he swung a skinny arm to the east—"and they was both signals. I'm going up the coulée to scout. You tried to betray me into the hands of my enemies, but I'll protect yuh. I want a whole box of shells, and the Bowie knife." He indicated the old broken-handled butcher knife that Cliff used mostly for paring potatoes and slicing bacon.

Cliff absently nodded assent, and reached to the eaves for the box of revolver cartridges. "Don't go pointing toward any stock," he warned mechanically, "and don't carry your gun

cocked. Yuh might fall down and blow your head off. Don't
yuh lose that knife, either." With that, he absolved himself
mentally from responsibility for accidents, and relapsed into
deep meditation.

When the boy was gone to his play, Cliff got paper and a
bottle that held a black sediment he called ink, and searched
in the cigar box of poker chips, buttons, and nails for his pen.
"Maybe she won't be none glad to hear from me . . . not if she
feels the way she did when I left . . . but I'm going to write
anyhow, for luck. I guess she must 'a' worried some about the
kid, and so. . . ." He found the pen, discovered the points
crossed and broke them in trying to straighten them, swore
absent-mindedly, hunted up the stubby pencil that he kept
for pinochle scores, and wrote painstakingly for an hour.

Then he went out and saddled Rocket, galloped hurriedly
out to the county road, and was just in time to catch the stage
driver and give him the letter and a two-bit piece in lieu of a
stamp.

That night when The Terror returned, Cliff eyed him
speculatively. "Kid, I been thinking yuh might as well settle
down and learn something useful. I feel kinda responsible for
the way yuh pan out . . . and, if yuh keep this gait, yuh won't
amount to nothing at all. So yuh got to quit hunting Indians
that ain't there, and learn to cook your own grub, and throw a
loop straight, and ride hosses, and such. I'll learn yuh to read
brands and . . . and milk," he finished lamely, seeing that the
offer was not meeting the enthusiasm it merited. "You're getting too big to play all the time," he went on persuasively.
"What yuh got to do, first off, is forget all about them stories
you've been reading and swallowing whole. There ain't anything to 'em. There never was no such a fellow as Daniel
Boone . . . and, if there was, he wouldn't uh lasted long. Yuh
can learn a lot out here . . . how to be the right kind uh man. If

yuh want to stay and your folks are willing, I'll do the best I can by yuh. But yuh got to settle down and quit all this Daniel Boone foolishness. I'll make yuh a heap more of a man than what he was. And it's the little things that count, so yuh can start right in. Yuh can wash up the dishes. Dishes have got to be washed, if yuh want to keep clean and decent. It may be kinda unpleasant, but it's necessary."

Washing dishes did not appeal to The Terror as belonging properly to Western life as he wished to live it. But once his mind was settled upon a thing, Cliff Wayne was rather a firm young man. There were words—even a tear or so, knuckled hastily into oblivion—but The Terror washed the dishes. After that, he sulked.

"Another thing," Cliff began again without preface the next morning. "I'm going to give yuh a decent, respectable name . . . one that wouldn't make your . . . a fellow's sister ashamed to hear him called by. It ain't any particular credit to a man to be called a terror. You ain't one. You're just a kinda ornery kid that needs a heap uh training. I . . . I knew a girl once that had a little brother . . . and he was named Thaddeus. It's a queer name. She didn't call him that, though. She called him Tad. He was about six years old when I saw him last, and. . . ." He struck a match sharply along the wall beside him where he sat at table. "Kid, I'm going to call yuh Tad."

The Terror, new christened, looked startled. One might say that he looked genuinely frightened for a moment. He watched Cliff while the latter puffed leisurely at his cigarette, but he did not say anything—and he was the sort of boy who usually has a retort ready to his tongue.

"We'll leave the dishes go till noon," said Cliff, breaking a silence that had grown uncomfortable. "The fence is down up at the head uh the little field. Yuh get the bucket uh staples and the hammer, and come along and help . . . and learn how to do it. I'll make a rancher outta yuh, Tad."

Tad did not want to be a rancher. He did not like to hold up barbed wire against a post while Cliff drove in the staples, or to hold the pointed stakes while Cliff pounded upon the top to send them securely into the dry sod. Most of all he did not want to learn anything useful; that, primarily, had been his chief reason for running away from home.

But Cliff was different these days. He did not hand out his gun and shells to The Terror for the sake of peace and quiet, and he did not tell The Terror to "go on off, and not bother the life plumb out of a man." He seemed to feel a new responsibility, and to be disconcertingly zealous in the thorough performance of his self-imposed duty. He was eternally finding something useful which the boy must learn to do, and do well. He labored whole days to teach him the art of making sourdough bread, and of washing dishes so that they would not have a polish of grease.

The Terror—who Cliff called Tad—formed a habit of staring resentfully at nothing at all, and of sitting through the long evenings sulkily, refusing to talk, or even to answer when Cliff spoke to him.

One morning Cliff awoke to find him gone—gone upon Rocket, at that—and with him Cliff's revolver, all the cartridges in the house, and the field glass. For a time, Cliff believed that he had merely slipped away to play his favorite game, and he called himself several hard things for expecting a boy of twelve to settle down all at once and become a man. He had not permitted him once to go up the coulée hunting Indians, or even to play stage robber and hold up the hayrick out by the corral.

When he was cleaning up after breakfast, however, he discovered the absence of certain things that did not look quite like play. A whole strip of bacon was gone, a fifty-cent package of matches, half a sack of flour, and all the tea, besides a frying pan, some blankets, and a few trifling objects which would appeal to a boy. When he found that the pasture gate had been opened wide and that all the horses were gone save the one that the boy had ridden into the country, Cliff's sense of responsibility changed to personal resentment. He saddled the remaining horse, and set out to find The Terror.

The mount he had was what he would have called a "bench", a worn-out saddle horse with stiffened joints and a tendency to wheeze if one galloped him farther than a furlong without breaking the pace. Still, with an angry man in the saddle, he traveled faster than usual, and he had carried Cliff ten miles or more when they met the first man who might be questioned. But the man, when Cliff rode close and opened his mouth for speech, developed a surprising greed for information on his own account. He stared in unfriendly fashion, and asked Cliff where he had got that M-S horse, and if he could show a bill of sale for him.

Cliff stiffened in the saddle, scented trouble, and did some rapid thinking. When a man meets another upon the open range and questions that other's title to the horse he is astride, there is usually more to come.

"He don't belong to me," Cliff admitted. "I . . . I just borrowed him. . . ."

"And I'll just borrow your company for a while," cut in the other. "I'm stock inspector, and I've got orders to take in that M-S horse and the fellow that stole him. We'll ride back to town, if you ain't got any objections."

Cliff had, and he stated them as calmly as was possible, considering the mood he was in. He gave his name, occupation, and what other details might help him, and he generously refrained from mentioning The Terror. He could not, he assured himself, get the kid into trouble even if he were a little liar and a little thief, and a few other immoral things. He took the trail to town and rode moodily beside the inspector, wishing that he had never seen The Terror, or that, having seen him, he had not tried to make a man of him and written his optimistic plans to the girl, Tad's sister.

It was when they were passing a roadhouse ten miles out from town that Cliff jarred back to present realities. The stage was drawn up at the gate a little way from the trail, and the driver was just going up the steps to the saloon door. In the front seat of the rig, holding the reins with manifest nervousness, sat a woman—a young woman, if one might judge from her poise and slender figure.

Cliff, divining much in the glance he gave, jerked his horse down to a walk. "That's Joe Donovan driving stage today," he said to the inspector. "And he never was known to make the trip sober. I . . . I think I know the lady. I'd like to stop and tell her not to go on with him. I won't be more'n a minute."

"Yuh won't be that long," grunted the inspector, pulling his horse around to block Cliff's way. "We've got nothing to do with the stage, or who drives it, or who rides in it. We're headed for town. Come on."

For a moment, Cliff meditated attacking an officer of the law. Then he saw how useless it would be with the inspector carrying a gun and legal immunity, and himself having no weapon, and apparently a very good cause for wishing for freedom. He thought of trying to persuade the other—and gave up that idea, also. The inspector did not look susceptible to chivalrous impulses, although he did look determined to land his prisoner in jail with the least possible delay. Cliff shrugged his shoulders, hoped that he had been mistaken in the identity of the girl, and rode obediently on down the trail.

Still, the incident clung to his thoughts, troubling him

more than did his own predicament. Once in town, he could
—and did—speedily release himself from custody of the law.
Men knew him and willingly vouched for him, so that within
an hour he was out on a cash bail, and had borrowed a horse
that had the speed that Cliff felt his mission required. He
even neglected to ask if any had seen The Terror ride that
way; he had forgotten the boy, so greatly was his mind troubled about another matter. He hurriedly thanked his
bondsmen, scowled at the inspector, rode to the stage office,
and told them briefly what he thought of them for sending Joe
Donovan out with the stage and a lone woman passenger. He
asked her name, discovered that they did not know anything
about her except that she had come in on the morning train
and seemed in a hurry to reach Cliff Wayne's ranch and,
when he heard the last sentence, put spurs to his horse and
left town on a run.

At the roadhouse he stopped long enough to find that the
stage had been gone from there an hour or more, and that Joe
had "tanked up" pretty well. The girl had held the horses
while Joe was inside, and had gone on with him. Cliff was so
perturbed that he did not even wait long enough to curse the
stolid Dutchman who kept the house and who told him all
this in a matter-of-fact way that would have been maddening
if Cliff had not been in such haste.

He jammed his foot in the stirrup, went up, and landed in
the saddle, jabbing the spurs in at the instant when his heels
came within reach of his horse. He pulled his hat down to his
eyebrows that the wind might not take it from him, made a
mechanical effort to button his coat, gave up the attempt
after the first failure to locate the button he wanted, and left
the coat flapping in the wind.

The Dutchman stood in the doorway and watched him
stupidly. "Py cosh, he iss in one big hurry about somet'ings,"

he remarked to his dog, and went heavily in and shut the door.

Cliff galloped to the upper rim of Skull Coulée where the trail wound down through scant patches of brush to the flat bottomland. Where the banks crept closest to the trail, he saw the stage standing empty, the horses cramping the wheels to one side while they nibbled at some tender twigs. He felt instinctively for his gun, remembered that The Terror had taken it, and turned sick with fear that was not for himself.

When he plunged headlong around the last curve and was close, the sudden shift from anxiety to relief turned him weak and swaying in the saddle. The girl was safe enough, apparently. She was standing with her veil tucked up under her hat and her back against a rock, looking away up the farther hillside.

Cliff slid from the saddle, felt his knees bend under him, and threw an arm over the reeking neck of his horse. One would have thought from the way he was panting that he had made that last half mile on foot.

The girl turned her head, gave him a startled look, and relaxed visibly. "Oh . . . is it Cliff Wayne? I . . . you are Cliff, aren't you? Your eyes haven't changed. . . ." She took a step or two toward him, holding out her hand with a pretty indecision. "Such a country!" She laughed in a hysterical way, as if it would be quite as easy to cry. "Here's my driver acting the queerest . . . I think he's . . . er . . . intoxicated. He could scarcely stay in the rig when we went over bumps. And here's Tad"— she waved her tan-gloved arm up the hillside—"holding us up . . . with a real gun, mind you! And the driver seems to be taking him quite seriously. He jumped from the wagon and ran for dear life up the hill, and Tad ran after him, waving the gun and shouting stagey things. I thought you wrote that you had reformed Tad. Or were going to, or some. . . ."

111

It took Cliff just that long to get a grip on himself. He let go the horse and lurched toward her.

She backed up. "Oh, have you been drinking, too?"

Cliff laughed uncertainly. He steadied himself, and caught her in his arms. "I'm sure glad to see you, girl," he said, holding her tightly. "I just didn't expect to see you, that's all. I . . . I didn't mean for you to come. . . ."

"Oh, if you didn't want me. . . ." She blushed, and wriggled resentfully in his arms. "Let me go then. I can take Tad and go home. I. . . ."

Cliff laughed. "No, yuh can't. Pretty soon I'll explain what I meant by that. I sure didn't mean that I don't want you. I do. I'm going to keep yuh. You kinda surprised me, coming out unexpected like this, when the most I hoped for was a letter . . . but I like to be surprised, girlie. I. . . ."

Shouting from the hillside interrupted a lot of foolishness. It was The Terror, standing upon a rock, yelling down to them. Cliff turned that way, and the girl took to patting her hair and straightening her hat.

"I guess I'll have to go up there and see what the kid's up to," he said reluctantly, and left her.

Presently he returned, half dragging the stage driver, who was shedding maudlin tears over his woes.

The Terror strutted proudly beside them, explaining breathlessly. "I was going to hold him up," he admitted unblushingly. "I'm a stage robber. I watched 'em coming through the field glass, and then I seen there was a lady. Daniel Boone wouldn't hurt a lady. And then I seen the stage driver was acting funny and drunk, and so I rescued the lady, and. . . . Gee! I never knowed it was you, Carrots!" The Terror looked as if he meditated flight. "What'd yuh go and wear that thick veil on your face for? Gee!" Amazement grew on his face. "How'd yuh know . . . ?"

112

"Never mind that now," Cliff said. "You go and pile onto Rocket, and come along back to town. No . . . I'll go with you. Bring him here, and tie him behind the stage. He'll lead, all right. I've got a matter uh private business I want to see yuh about, young man. No"—he smiled reassuringly into the girl's questioning eyes—"it ain't . . . serious. I . . . you want him to come to the wedding, don't yuh?"

That stopped her questions, and left her quite occupied with her confusion and her thoughts, so that Cliff felt justified in leaving her alone for a few minutes while he followed The Terror to the clump of brush where Rocket was hidden from sight. He stated his matter of business abruptly and without pity, and was stopped by The Terror's vehement denial of the charge.

"I never, either! I never stole nothing but . . . but Rocket and the gun and stuff . . . and I was mad at you, and wanted to get even. I never stole that horse. I bought him from a kid that said his father give it to him. I'll go back with yuh and prove it. I paid him twenty-five dollars that I got for my wheel. He was a fellow about twenty, and he lived on a ranch about two miles from Glasgow. I can take yuh right to the place. You . . . you needn't believe me . . . I can prove it. I. . . ."

The Terror was shedding the real tears of childhood, and Cliff believed. Later his belief was fully justified.

"Well, that's all right, then. I can easy fix things up, if you can find the fellow yuh bought him from. Chances are he's the one the inspector really wants . . . not me or you. Come on, now . . . we've got to go back to town and have a wedding, kid. I'm going to be your brother-in-law . . . and, then, you bet I'll make yuh mind!"

When they were almost within hearing of the girl who waited, Cliff looked down again at The Terror, who was knuckling his eyes industriously beside him. "And see here,

Tad . . . you mustn't call my wife Carrots. Her name's Carrie. *¿Sabe?*"

"Aw, she ain't your wife!"

"She will be before dark. Climb in on the back seat where you can keep an eye on Rocket . . . and you, too, Joe . . . if you ain't aiming to lay out here all night. Come, girlie."

The Problem

Appearing in *The Popular Magazine* (8/1/10), "The Problem" was the first of a series about the Lady Slipper outfit in Northern Montana. Alcohol addiction was a common problem on the range, presented here with a surprising and dramatic twist. Brant Whipple, a valuable Lady Slipper hand, is useless when he is drunk, but he can't seem to leave the joy juice alone. The outfit heads a big shipping herd toward the railroad where all hands will be needed, and Brant's thirst gets the better of him again. When all hell breaks loose, he is both the cause and an instrument of fickle fate. The vivid description of the cattle drive, the outfit's camp, and subsequent events show Bower's knowledge of a process few women authors could even imagine. She also proved with this series that B. M. Bower's popularity did not depend entirely on humor.

A low-hanging dust cloud trailed far out behind and in front obscured all save the big, swaying bodies and rhythmically swinging heads of the leaders as the beef herd toiled up the last heart-breaking hill. Slowly they crawled out on the level of the bench land that bordered the big flat where would be the last sleep upon their native soil before the evil-smelling stock cars hurried them away to the ultimate justification of their existence.

Back on the drag where the dust was thickest, Brant Whipple choked, coughed, and swore at the hindmost steer—dabbled futilely at his aching, bloodshot eyes and

115

wished by all the gods he knew and could invoke in four lan-
guages that he was well away from the dust and the cattle that
ground it out from the prairie sod—wished he was quenching
his thirst in the town, which even then could be plainly seen
by the men riding point.

"Before I take a deal like this again for any blame temper-
ance boss on the face of this green earth, may I. . . ." He was
off on one of those long, blisteringly profane flights of a disturbed cowpuncher's imagination, a flight picturesquely
daring, vividly blasphemous.

The foreman, who had stopped half a mile back to gossip
with a ranch owner on his way home from town, galloped up,
heard a little of what Brant was declaiming to the four winds
and any man who cared to listen, grinned, and passed on
along the long line of cattle to the point.

Brant scowled after him and stopped swearing long
enough to grumble coherently to the man nearest him: "He's
so blamed scared I might want to ride into town for a minute
or two, I reckon he put me on day herd out uh my turn, just so
he can keep cases on me. Why, *I* ain't going to tank up this
trip. I know where I can get plenty of it. But I don't want it. I
ain't got any intentions uh drinking anything . . . unless,
maybe, it's a glass uh beer. I swore off three weeks ago yesterday. I ain't had a drop since then."

The listener coughed behind his hand to hide a grin.
Three weeks ago yesterday the Lady Slipper had pulled out
from town after shipping a trainload of beef, and it had pulled
out with Brant Whipple riding in the bed wagon, too drunk to
sit up. The listener had been one of the men who had, with
much labor, loaded Brant into the wagon and made
sure—with a rope or two—that he could not fall out deliberately or accidentally. For Brant Whipple, drunk, was ever dis-
orderly and not to be depended upon even when he was

asleep. Sober, he was conceded to be one of the best men in the outfit—and the Lady Slipper was not running a crew of pilgrims, either.

"It'll be all the same a hundred years from now," philosophized Brant's listener not too originally. "We'll all be in town tomorrow night, anyhow, if they've got the cars . . . and I guess they have, all right."

Brant gave an unmollified grunt. "Tomorrow ain't today . . . nor tonight, either. What I hate, Bill, is to have folks always expecting me to break out. Why, blast that fool Lockie's heart, I didn't have no intentions uh going to town till tomorrow . . . but he shoved me on herd just to keep me out uh sight uh the burg as long as he could, just as if that would stop me, if I wanted to go bad enough!"

He stood in his stirrups and gazed longingly ahead over the ripple of broad backs and swore again because the dust shut out the town from his straining sight. "You know blamed well, Bill," he complained, settling back, "that ain't any way to treat a man."

"Well, you don't have to stay on the drag and take all the dust there is, if yuh don't want to," Bill reminded him bluntly. "Why don't yuh get up front? You can likely see town if yuh ride point a while. And you don't want to take Lockie too personal. Somebody had to go on out uh turn this afternoon, with Owlie sick."

"Sick . . . nothin'!" snorted Brant. "That was just a plant. And anyway," he added, "it didn't have to be me."

Bill gave up the argument and swung back to bring up a straggler, for they were not grazing the herd along that afternoon. Instead, they were pushing them ahead with what speed they might, because the mid-summer dry spell had made water scarce and a long drive absolutely necessary to reach the next creek, which was close to town.

Privately Bill considered that the foreman had shown a good deal of wisdom in putting Brant on day herd, instead of Owlie. Brant would have to stand guard that night—probably the middle guard, if he still took Owlie's place. That would leave him little opportunity to ride into town and slake his thirst at the expense of his brains and the working capacity of the Lady Slipper.

If he had been left to his regular routine, Brant would have been lying around camp at that very minute, instead of martyring himself in the dust of the drag. He would have had the short guard at the tail end of the afternoon, and at dusk he would have been free from duty until the morning, and with town no more than a thirty-mile gallop away it was easy to guess what Brant would have done with those hours of freedom.

Bill mentally went over the situation and the well-known weakness of his companion, and decided that Owlie's sudden indisposition had been too opportune to be genuine. Under the present arrangement, Brant would have no leisure, save the two or three hours of lying around camp after the herd had been thrown on water, and the few hours of sleep before he would be called for guard. In the morning the whole outfit would be at work, and they would keep moving until the last steer was crowded into the last car and the door fastened after him. After that, there would be others beside Brant Whipple racing eagerly to where they might quench their thirst.

"We'll be on water in another hour, and outta this dust!" Bill cheered, when he came back within loud talking distance of Brant.

Brant made no reply whatever. He was riding sullenly, with both hands clasped upon the saddle horn, one foot swinging free of its stirrup and a cigarette between his lips. His hat was pulled down over his frowning brows, his eyes were half closed in a squint against the smothering dust that had made his face as gray as his hat, and his whole attitude spoke eloquently of the mood he was in.

Not once during the remainder of that drive did he open his lips, except when he freed his lungs of smoke, coughed because of the dust, or swore at a straggler. Bill was not without tact, although he was young in range lore and still had enthusiasm for the life. Not even the discomforts of riding on the drag with twelve hundred marching beef cattle kicking dust into his face on a hot, windless day could wither this enthusiasm.

He did not attempt to win Brant to speech, which was wise. At the same time, Bill, with his healthy young animal desires and appetites and energy, while he recognized the unpleasant mood of the other, could not quite understand it, or grasp the terrible influence of the thirst devil when it grips a tired man who has not for three weeks of hard work tasted any stimulant stronger that coffee.

To Bill it was a matter for unobtrusive amusement—this longing that Brant showed for town. Bill guessed that Brant would have to be hauled out in the bed wagon again, and would want to fight every man who came near him during the sobering process, but it was no concern of his.

They'd have all kinds of excitement, very likely, and Lockie, the foreman, would once more threaten to can Brant, as he had done the last time, and the time before that, and other times that had passed into the history of the Lady Slipper. It was merely one of those incidents that have not the charm of novelty, except when they fail to happen. If, for instance, Brant Whipple should by some miracle go through with a shipping without getting drunk, the Lady Slipper would be all agog with wonder and speculation.

The herd, bellowing thirstily, poured down the long, steep

slope to the sluggish grass-clogged creek at the mouth of a narrow coulée that opened abruptly into a great flat basin, at the other side of which slumped the town. Two hundred yards or so up the creek, the tents of the Lady Slipper were showing their familiar blotch of gray-white against the brown grass, with a scanty fringe of dispirited willows making a wavering line of green along the creek bank. Never twice in the same setting, those two tents were home to the men of the Lady Slipper—a goal to be reached thankfully always, be it day or night, hot or cold, wet or dry.

Bill's eyes brightened at the sight, and he cleared his throat of the last clinging particles of dust, untied and shook vigorously his neckerchief, and hailed joyfully the two men ambling leisurely out from camp to relieve them. Others would follow—others were following, even then—to take charge of the herd. The two who came first rode straight toward Bill and Brant Whipple, and they swung their horses to meet them.

"Hot, ain't it?" one of them called out, carelessly voicing the obvious, as is the way of men who have nothing of importance to say. "Weather breeder, if you ask *me*."

"Well, if it holds off till we get these cattle off our hands, it'll suit me fine," Bill replied good-naturedly.

"Bet you'll be trying to find more buttons on your slickers tonight, you fellows." The other grinned as they met and passed on. "Glad *I* don't have to stand guard tonight!"

Brant scowled at him and grunted, for this was pressing close upon a grievance that, with the town in plain sight, was becoming bitter.

"Bet I don't stand guard, either," he muttered.

But Bill had put his horse to a gallop that he might reach camp a second or two sooner, and failed to hear the covert threat.

At the corral, when he rode slowly up, Lockie was speaking loudly to someone.

"No, sir! The man that rides to town before this beef is loaded can take his bed along with him. The cars are there, waiting, and I ain't going to round up a bunch uh drunken 'punchers before I start working the herd in the morning."

Brant's lip curled as he dismounted and began loosening the latigo. He believed that the warning, while ostensibly given to another, was aimed at himself alone. That was the way with Lockie—always hitting at you over another man's shoulder.

Brant thought that Lockie would have been wiser and would have gained more surely his object, if he had come to him straight and asked him—or even ordered him to stay in camp and out of the way of temptation. This sly maneuvering, his putting Brant on herd out of his turn, and warning others, when he meant Brant alone, was a fool's way of managing a man.

Brant shot an angry, sidelong glance at his foreman while he threw his saddle on the ground. It was then that the spirit of revolt was born within him.

He ate his supper in silence, although other men chatted around him. Afterward, he lay in the shade and smoked moodily until it was time to catch and saddle his night horse, which he did with a certain sullen determination.

He looped up the long, free end of his latigo, unhooked the stirrup from the horn and let it drop with a snap, which sent his horse leaping sidewise. Brant jerked him to a snorting stand, led him out away from the corral and bed tent instead of tying him to the wagon as he should have done, pulled his hat down upon his head for swift riding, and mounted without a word to anyone.

"Here! Where yuh going?" called Lockie hastily, starting toward him.

Brant, already in the saddle, turned his spurs toward his horse's body and grinned at Lockie over his shoulder. "Going for my mail. I'll be back in a little while!" He was off before Lockie could choose a reply.

"His mail!" the foreman spluttered angrily, gazing after Brant's fleeing figure. "Like thunder he's after his mail! Ain't had any mail since I knew him!" He stood irresolute, as if he were mediating a chase. "I reckon he thinks I'll haul him outta town again in the bed wagon and sober him up. . . ."

Then, realizing how unwise it is for a foreman to speak his mind freely about erring, absent ones, he went into the bed tent and unrolled his bed. Brant would be howling drunk before midnight—that was a foregone conclusion. By morning he would be unable to sit in the saddle, much less read brands and help work the herd preparatory to loading the cattle. The Lady Slipper, already working with too small a crew, would be shy another man—and that man one of the best. The foreman spread his blankets, decided that the tent was too sultry a place to sleep, and dragged his bed out under the mess wagon.

Other men were deserting their canvas shelter in spite of the threatening west, for the air was stifling even after the sun had ceased to redden the sky. Later, they believed, there would be rain, perhaps wind, certainly plenty of thunder and lightning if one might judge by the purple bank of clouds that hung low upon the skyline. Perhaps the threatening storm would pass them by, as so many storms lately had done, leaving their range still thirsting for rain. So with shelter or without it, as the heat and fancy dictated, the Lady Slipper outfit slept with the deep unheeding slumber of work-wearied men.

All, that is, save the night guards riding slowly around and around their sleeping charge. By sound they rode mostly, by that unerring instinct born of intimate knowledge and long habit. So dark it was that they could not see one another when they met and passed on, and only their voices singing, and the faint, telltale whisper of saddle leather, the mouthing of a bit, the subdued rattle of bridle chains bore evidence to each of the proximity of the other. So still it was that the sigh of an uneasy steer came clearly to Bill on the far side of the herd.

Bill was young and inclined toward romance. He liked the blackness of the night and the mysterious quiet of all nature. Even the frogs over in the creek seemed to croak diffidently, as if they hesitated to spoil the silence. It seemed to Bill that the world was seeing how long it could hold its breath, and that the night was a black-cloaked woman, treading softly a-tiptoe over the sleeping earth. Bill was given to dreaming poetical things that he would never have dared put into words.

When a fellow across the herd began singing—or rather crooning—in the monotonous drone of a cowboy folk song, Bill turned his head and listened, his nerves aquiver.

Oh, bury me not on the lone prairie,
Where the wild coyotes will howl o'er me,
Where the rattlesnakes hiss and the wind goes free. . . .

Bill knew the song—many's the time he had sung it unremittingly from start to finish, with that same chorus plaintively wailed between the verses. He had never thought much about it before, but had sung and heard it sung unthinkingly. It was a sentimental thing, not founded upon reality or common sense. When a cowboy's light went out—according to the testimony of the living—he didn't give a darn what they did to him or where they buried him. But in the velvet blackness of that night, the words lost their maudlin sentimentality and came to Bill with pulsing earnestness.

> **Oh, bury me not on the lone prairee!**
> **Oh, bury me where a mother's prayer**
> **And a sister's tears may mingle there . . .**
> **Where my friends may come and weep o'er me.**

In the sanity of daylight the singer was not given to longing for the prayers or tears of anybody on earth. He was an unemotional cowpuncher with a touchy past, a vivid vocabulary, and no sentiment that went deeper than his horse's and his own animal instincts. But his voice, when he sang in the night, had a plaintive, pleading note that lifted Bill out of reality and into the world of waking dreams.

> **Oh, bury me not on the lone prairee!**
> **Oh, bury me not . . . but his voice failed there,**
> **And they gave no heed to his dying prayer.**
> **In a narrow grave just six by three,**
> **And they buried him there on the lone prairee.**
> **Oh-h, bury me not on the lone prairie!**
> **Oh-h, bury me not on the lone prairee. . . .**

The singer was riding toward him, but it was not the soft, padding sound of his horse's hoofs that made a steer close to Bill snort and begin shuffling to rise, rump first, to look and listen. Bill forgot the heart-gripping plaint of the song and listened and looked, also. Almost overhead, the clouds brightened with the sullen flare of hidden lightning, but the rumble that went with it was faint, and not disquieting.

Off in the night somewhere was a sound of galloping—the pattering beat of hoofs. Unerringly, led by some malicious instinct, they neared the herd. Bill, mindful of the cattle, turned and rode to meet and warn the comer.

"Hold on!" he cried cautiously, as if he feared to wake a sleeping child. "You'll be on top of the herd in another minute!"

A shrill, reckless yell answered him: "*A-yee-e-e-ipp!* That's what I want . . . the herd. Gotta stand guard. Hello, bossies! What . . . ?"

With a clashing of horns, the herd was up and away like flushed quail. There was no warning, no preparation for flight, no hesitation as to direction or leadership. That first yell had brought them to their feet as one animal and away, and the night was no longer still with an ominous quiet. It was roaring with the rushing, mad, never-to-be-forgotten clamor of a stampede.

A few steers bawled suddenly, throatily—they were the ones that were a fraction of a second late in getting to their feet, and they were paying the penalty under the lunging bodies of those that stumbled over them. For the herd, taking fright at the edge toward Brant Whipple and the creek, had stampeded across its own bed ground.

There was some confusion, some crowding, here and there, a jumble of bodies where a steer had tripped, but the men on guard saw nothing of it, and even while they wheeled their horses for pursuit, the herd was gone, thundering away in the black darkness.

Brant Whipple, back from the town with a pint of whisky inside him and two quarts in his coat pockets, gave another drunken yell and emptied his six-shooter into the air as he galloped. "Go it!" he jeered, racing jubilantly after the herd. "Git a move on! You don't need no sleep, anyhow. What yuh want's . . . exercise . . . exercise! Git off the earth, you brutes!" He was cursing, laughing, urging them on, as if it were all a huge joke on the cattle.

In camp, Lockie, his ears and his nerves trained like soldiers always doing sentinel duty, heard and reached mechanically for his hat, stuck it on his head, and drew his clothes toward him while he yelled: "Boys! The cattle's running!"

Four words, but they brought every man back from dreamland. Each grabbed his clothes even while they were being uttered, and not one needed explanation or orders.

They jerked on their boots, stamped their feet into them on the way to where their horses were tied, freed them by the sense of touch alone, felt for stirrups in the darkness, mounted, and were off in the time a green hand would have consumed in rubbing the sleep from his eyes and trying to realize what had happened. Lockie found time to be thankful that the look of the west at sundown had made him order every man to saddle a night horse, so that none but the cook stayed in camp.

It is not good to let a beef herd take fright and stampede in the night, especially on the last night before being huddled in stuffy cars and sent rattling away to the East. Lockie looked at the quiet storm clouds—quiet, in comparison with the tumult they might have made—and wondered what had started the cattle. Then, above the fast-decreasing rumble of the stampede, he heard a long-drawn—"*Ah yee-e-e!*"—and the roar of a .45.

He dug his unspurred heels into his horse and swore aloud in his wrath: "It's that drunken fool of a Brant Whipple! And if I ever git my hands on him, and if he ever shows up at the Lady Slipper ag'in. . . . A man like that oughta be hung! Anybody that will shoot and yell at a beef herd on the bed ground had oughta. . . ."

His horse stumbled over a loose rock, recovered itself with a lurch, and went pounding on the faster to atone for the misstep. Lockie gave over the futile attempt to ease his feelings by mere words, however vitriolic. But it would have been unpleasant for Brant, had his foreman come within reach of him then.

By the sense of riding always up a slope while they followed the fleeing herd, they knew that they were running up out of the creek bottom to the bench land beyond. The foreman was glad of that, for the long, steep hill would, perforce, shorten their wind and cool their ardor for a race. He hoped that the night herders would be able to check them by the time they reached the level land above. But with that drunken maniac still letting out an occasional whoop that carried clearly back to those who followed, the outlook was not hopeful.

The storm was now overhead, and the thunder was muttering threats of what would come later. More frequently the lightning played behind the clouds, turning them all golden yellow with an occasional quick sword thrust of vivid flame. But it held off—more exactly, it seemed to be passing over to throw itself bodily against the rugged steeps of the mountains beyond. Lockie hoped that it would. He did not want to grapple with storm and stampede together.

They pounded up the last slope, their horses breathing asthmatically, and reached the level. There, before them, when the lightning lit for an instant the whole land, they saw the herd, a black blotch in the distance. There was no more yelling, no more shooting.

"He's cooled down mighty sudden, darn him!" said the foreman. He felt complacent that the thought of himself and his vengeance had at last penetrated the whisky-fogged brain of Brant and silenced him. "But I'll sure hand it to him for this!" he threatened vindictively.

Away on the ragged fringe of the herd rode Bill, the singer, and two other herders, turning back the leaders with shots, yells, and swinging loops to throw them into the rushing bulk. By the time the others arrived, the cattle were swinging to the left. In ten minutes or less the herd was running in a circle, doubling always back upon itself; a bit of that and they slowed to a walk, milling uneasily around and around. The stampede was stopped.

Lockie rode close. "Where's that idiot?" With many epithets, he indicated Brant.

"I dunno!" Bill called in reply. "We dropped him two miles back. He'd uh had us clear across into Dakota, I guess, if he'd kept up that yelling and trying to shoot the tails off the drag. He sure had us going!"

The foreman forgot the dignity and the discipline of silence and raved while he rode to help keep the cattle bunched. "I'd like to get my hands on him once," he finished grimly, and the men of the Lady Slipper joined him fervently in his desire. A cowboy is always jealous of his sleep—he gets so little of it, at the best.

The rain began to fall in little gusts of large, cool drops for which they were grateful after the heat. The thunder boomed, but it was now ahead, on the broken foothills, that the force of the storm was spent. The cattle were startled, but, with the full crew of the Lady Slipper to hold them there, they did nothing but mill around and around, their eyes wild and phosphorescently bright. In a few minutes the clouds trailed off in ragged streamers, torn by wind the earth did not feel. The moon showed the black cloud patches swimming rapidly.

The foreman thought then of his bed, and the few hours sleep which he might yet enjoy. Plainly the storm had passed them by with only a flirt or two of rain in their faces. With the moon shining, he could see the herd quieting down, so he doubled the guard, called the rest of his crew, and headed for camp again.

"Wind coming," announced a man tersely, when a great roaring came suddenly to their ears. The others turned their heads and listened.

"No . . . that ain't wind," Lockie contradicted after a minute, and swung into his saddle to look at the inky blackness to the east. He did not quite know what it was, although he had a somewhat hazy impression that it was the storm. Then he reined his horse sharply to one side and galloped away to the edge of the bluff where it hunched its barren shoulders close to the narrow coulée with the creek running through—the creek beside which rested the tents of the Lady Slipper.

"Sounds to me like water!" he shouted over his shoulder, and the others turned and followed him.

At the brink of the high bluff they pulled up short, and, with that sullen roar booming up to them, they looked below. In the fickle moonlight, blotted frequently by bits of a straying storm cloud, they could not see much—but they saw quite enough. Down below, where the creek had wandered aimlessly through a sparse line of willows, was a solid swirling wall of water. They could see it dimly lighted by the moon. They heard it go raving on down the narrow coulée, even while they stood there watching.

The foreman wheeled his horse and dashed off without a word, the others racing close alongside and behind. There was the camp and the cook, unwarned of the hurrying deluge. They knew there was little hope of outrunning that flood. Indeed, it passed them by in the first hundred yards of the race, but for that they hurried the faster.

When they reached the slope down which it was possible to ride, they knew it was too late. And as if the moon knew what they were about, it shone out brightly to show them the tragedy. For where the tents of the Lady Slipper had stood in the fringe of willows, there was nothing but black whirling water, with the willow tops dragging on the surface.

They halted there on the high ground. They had to halt or ride back upon the bench land, for the water barred the way in front. They did not say much—there was not much that they could say. One man said it was like a cloudburst he had seen once in Colorado, when a herd of cows and calves, lying "on water"—which means that they were taking their ease beside a stream—had drowned, and the herders had barely escaped with their lives. But that, he added, had been in daylight and had given them a chance to hit 'er up for high ground.

No one mentioned the cook. It did not seem to be necessary, for they all knew, almost in detail, what had happened when the water struck the camp.

At daylight, when the flood had passed, they found him lodged in a willow half a mile below. The night hawk, having fortunately chosen the cooler, high ground for his saddle bunch that night, brought down his herd of horses unscathed. They located the wagons, overturned and half buried in mud and débris, hauled them out with their ropes, and did what they could to repair the damage that had been done. The cook they laid out decorously upon a large, flat rock, and covered him with a sodden tarpaulin. Until they could do no more there in the creek bottom, no man spoke what was in the minds of all. Then Lockie, mounted upon a fresh horse, looked down the creek to where the cattle had laid at dusk.

"If the herd hadn't jumped the bed ground when they did," he said, "there wouldn't be one left to tell the tale this morning. It sure does beat thunder the way things happen sometimes." That set him to thinking of Brant Whipple. And because he was thinking of Brant, and of his sudden silence and disappearance the night before, he took up the trail of the stampede on his way out to the herd.

Just on the brow of the bluff they found him huddled on the ground. By the signs, his horse had fallen and thrown him. He had hurts that it would take the hospital surgeon to name, and in his coat pockets was a jumble of broken glass and an overpowering odor of whisky.

They turned him to an easier position, and Lockie stood looking down at him, still with the puzzled frown. Brant had broken all the unwritten laws of the range—but he had saved their lives and the lives of the cattle.

Lockie shivered perceptibly when he thought what would have happened if the herd had not run, and so brought them all out of their blankets and away from the creek.

"Owlie, you ride in and git a rig to haul him to town," he commanded, "and don't try and see how slow you can be, either. Git as easy-riding a rig as yuh can, and put a bed in it."

When Owlie had galloped away, the foreman stooped and shifted Brant's head a trifle, and his touch was very gentle. Then he stood up and reached for his tobacco and papers.

"He's going t' pull through, all right," he predicted, with the wisdom which comes of much experience with range accidents. "And I'm busted if I know whether to fire the son-of-a-gun for stampeding the herd, or raise his wages for saving the hull outfit." He shook his head slowly, as if he found the fine point in ethics altogether too much for him. "If he was dead, we'd call him a hero, and that would settle it. But he ain't dead, and he ain't going to be. He'll be around ready to ride ag'in in six weeks or so." He pinched out the blaze of his match, dropped the stub to the ground, and set his heel upon it. "It sure does beat thunder," he finished vaguely, "the way things happen."

A Throne for a Day

Bertha and Bill Sinclair often patronized Great Falls businesses on Central Avenue. Bill met friends like artist Charlie Russell for cards at the posh Mint or Silver Dollar saloons. Bertha favored a sweet shop farther east. This story turns her ironic humor on the city's culture, as the men of the Flying U find themselves in a similar locale rarely found in Westerns. The story appeared in the February 15, 1910 issue of *The Popular Magazine*. During discussion of a book at a Flying U camp—Bertha's cowboys were usually literate, unlike the stereotype—a careless boast becomes a bet, making Pink Perkins "king for a day". Sure that he can outfox the other boys and earn some money, Pink leads them into the unfamiliar and frightening territory, where a good time is eventually had by *almost* all. Brother John was modeled after beloved Methodist circuit preacher, Brother Van Orsdel, who served north central Montana for several decades.

The Happy Family of the Flying U was camped for a day within ten miles of Great Falls. They had just delivered six hundred young cows and calves to an ambitious dry-land farmer, and they felt they deserved whatever joy the town might afford, which lay under the long wreath of smelter smoke. Just as soon as Patsy gave them their dinner, they meant to ride in and collect the joy, but, while they waited, they discussed the merits of a battered, paperbound classic they had found in a deserted sheep camp. It was a book dealing with kings and queens and personages of the Middle

Ages. They all liked it very much.

"The only thing that grinds me," observed Percival Cadwallader Perkins—who men called Pink—"is the way everyone in the bunch overlooked bets when they were riding point. What the first queen done, they all did, only a heap more mild. I wish to Josephine I'd had a whack at their throne. I'll gamble I'd have kept 'em going for one day, anyway."

"What all would yuh have done, Cadwolloper?" asked Weary.

"A dandy-fine king you'd make, Pink!" said Weary's double, who was called Irish.

"Aw, I betcha Pink wouldn't uh done a thing but keep them dimples uh his working and roll his eyes at the girls," put in Happy Jack in his usual pessimistic manner. "When a fellow's pretty, about all the hard work he'd do kingin' is to keep his crown on straight and watch the girls love him."

"What'll yuh bet?" Pink demanded sharply. Although he had the face of a tanned angel, he had not the temper of one, and he disliked having his good looks made the subject of conversation . . . especially by the Happy Family.

"Well," Happy Jack said, "I don't see no use of betting anything. You ain't a king."

"By gracious, let's make him one!" proposed Andy Green. "We can try him out as a king, all right, for a day. I believe in giving folks a chance to show what's in 'em. What do yuh say, boys?"

There were arguments for and against the proposition. They ended in a few heated sentences and some events as follows:

"If I had the running uh this bunch for a day," declared Pink, when they had goaded him almost to the fighting point, "I'll gamble there ain't one of yuh would have the nerve to follow my trail!"

"Say, we'll just *call* yuh, by glory!" exclaimed Big Medicine. "Git a crown, boys . . . we'll boost him up on the throne and let him do his damnedest, *on one condition!*" he roared, his face close to the face of Pink, his pale eyes standing out more frog-like than ever. "Tomorrow morning at sunup, little one, yuh pay five dollars to every fellow that stays with yuh and keeps the pace yuh set till the end. Un'erstand?"

"It's a go with me," Pink said with a smile, his irritation vanishing before the promise of deviltry. "With another condition . . . and that is every one of yuh that throws up his hands and quits the game pays *me* five dollars!"

Vociferously they agreed, after Slim and Happy Jack had been assured that there would be no royal beheadings or hangings or anything unpleasantly personal connected with the reign of Pink. They crowned Pink solemnly with a bit of buckbrush, and Weary told him to: "Go to it, Cadwolloper." Then they waited expectantly for results, and even suggested things.

At first, Pink did nothing but eat his dinner, and afterward seek a shady spot by the bed wagon and roll a cigarette, which he smoked in haughty silence.

"Aw, gwan!" urged Happy Jack, after an intolerable period of inaction. "Hurry up and git to kingin', why don't yuh?"

"It's a long time till sunup, Happy," Pink said imperturbably. "You'll likely get all the kingin' yuh want." He finished his cigarette with maddening deliberation before he spoke again. "Saddle up, boys," he told them. "We're going to town."

"That's dead easy!" cried Cal Emmett jubilantly. "We'll give yuh a steady job being king, Pink."

Pink smiled and carefully ground his cigarette stub into the dirt.

★ ★ ★ ★ ★

It is doubtful whether Pink had any definite plan for the defeat and humiliation of his fellows when they crossed the bridge and galloped up First Avenue between the parks that were showing a dainty green in the treetops, with long rows of tulips just coming into their full glory of bloom. He turned sharply at the first corner, led them clattering up past the depot, and around the curving driveway by the dry fountain onto Central Avenue.

"Aw . . . I betcha he's going to shoot up the town and git us all run in and fined," Happy Jack said suspiciously.

Pink deigned no reply whatever.

They neared a beer sign. "Say, king, how's chances for refreshments?" Irish insinuated thirstily.

"Couldn't be beat," replied Pink with a grin, and kept straight on down the street at a lope.

The face of Irish grew dejected, but the eyes of the king lit up suddenly to a glow of inspiration. He pulled up at the next corner and went slowly, glancing sharply at the places he passed. Behind him rode eight curious cowpunchers who watched him narrowly from under their hat brims. Bizarre, indeed, must be his reign if he would make those eight cry quits.

Midway down the next block he drew in to the curbstone. "Dismount, vassals," he cried as chestily as his vocal chords would permit. "Hold on there," he added as Irish headed instinctively for the nearest thirst emporium. "*I'm* riding herd on this bunch today."

Irish backed and waited restively while the others sought iron rings in the sidewalk where they might tie their horses solidly with their ropes. "If yuh knew how dry I am on the inside . . . ," he complained feelingly.

When they were all quite ready, Pink led the way to the

135

swinging doors of the saloon, turned just on the threshold, and walked away down the street. If he hoped by that means to shake off one or two members of his train, he was disappointed. The temptation was strong, but even Irish merely hesitated and clicked his teeth together before he followed their leader. Pink went to another saloon, then turned back.

"So that's your game, is it?" muttered Cal Emmett resentfully.

Still Pink said nothing. He went on down the street until he drew near a shining place where the windows were trimmed prettily with wide yellow ribbons and great fragrant bunches of cut daffodils, where women fluttered in and out through the door like hummingbirds in a lilac bush in May. He paused there, glanced wickedly back at his followers—still there were eight—and led the way straight up to the plateglass door, swung it nonchalantly open, and stood aside to let them pass through.

"After you, king," said Andy Green, and Pink went in.

The Happy Family gasped. "Well, by golly!" cried Slim aloud, purple to ears and collar. They entered, solemnly punctilious about removing their hats, glancing neither to right nor left, feeling in every quivering nerve the meaning of the blank cessation of sound, knowing without lifting their eyes that three or four dozen slim-handled silver spoons were being poised motionless in gloved fingers, and that eyes— feminine eyes—were regarding them with amazement.

"You little devil!" whispered Irish vindictively in the ear of his king when he overtook him.

Straight down the center of the long room marched Pink. With rowels buzzing and spur chains clanking and leaving marks upon the polished floor, the Happy Family grimly followed.

Pink drew out a chair at a vacant table as near the axis of

the shocked circle of femininity as if he had actually measured the room for that purpose, waved a gloved hand toward another table nearby, and watched with dancing eyes and dimples standing deeply in his cheeks while the men seated themselves. There were chairs for four at each table—and there were nine crimson-featured cowpunchers hurrying to find temporary sanctuary at tables.

Happy Jack, gulping at his tongue, was left stranded alone with women, women everywhere, look where he might. He shifted his weight from his right foot to his left, turned imploringly to his fellows, saw them grinning up at him with a lack of sympathy that seemed to him fiendish, and fled panic-stricken from the place.

The king, leaning back in the spindle-legged chair, raised the hand from which he had just drawn his glove, fingers and thumb outspread. He then moved his wrist and placed the index finger eloquently against his chest. The Happy Family read the pantomime accurately and with ease. It said: "Five dollars for mine." They grinned uncomfortably at one another, and stole surreptitious side glances at their whispering neighbors.

Great Falls, you must know, is rather self-conscious Eastern civilization snuggled picturesquely in a Western setting. It is progressive. It is boulevarded, parked, churched, and clubbed into perfect propriety. It receives ultimately much of the wealth that is gleaned from the cattle that roam the fast shrinking ranges to the north and east, but not often does it enjoy the sight of real cowboys garbed in the real working clothes of the rangeland.

When a cowboy goes to Great Falls for a holiday or a doctor or a dentist, he goes—putting it colloquially—in his war togs, which means high white collars, the best clothes he can buy, and a fresh haircut. His vocation is proclaimed only by his speech, his brown face and hands, and also by his walk, if one is observant and knows the type thoroughly. If by any chance he enters the town in chaps and spurs and riding restive horseflesh, he becomes the object of much attention. The Happy Family had not been unobserved in their passage down Central Avenue. Clerks and customers were still lingering just within doors, in hope of another glimpse.

It will be readily understood that their invasion of the candy shop most affected by the social elect created nothing short of a sensation. It was one of those rare spring days when the sunlight is soft and warm and the wind does not blow; there was a church fair next door, and a new-born club was being christened that day.

There were more than fifty well-gowned women in the shop, and they were all staring frankly at the Happy Family.

A pink-cheeked waitress came toward the men with evident trepidation to take their orders. The Happy Family gave her a hurried glance, and stared hard at the dull surface of the "mission-finished" tables. Only Pink and Irish had presence enough to grasp the menu cards.

The girl was waiting expectantly, self-consciously, coquettishly. The discomfort of the Happy Family grew with the passing seconds.

"Iscream!" blurted Slim in desperation, when he chanced to meet her eye.

Five other voices chorused the word. Irish, venturesome beyond his fellows and inspired by the long list of sundaes, said that he would try a Merry Widow Special, and Pink leaned back and grandly ordered Heavenly Hash. Those committed to plain ice cream perked their ears and stared at the two enviously.

Spoons began once more to clash musically against glass. Ice splinters tinkled coolly; soft voices murmured. Fifty women had remembered that it is not good form to stare. The faces of the Happy Family cooled gradually to their normal brown, their shoulders straightened to a more unconscious pose, their eyes wandered sometimes from their dishes and spoons.

"I'm going to have some uh that nutty truck, myself," declared Slim around his last mouthful of ice cream, staring at Pink's dish. "By golly, king's got to pay for it, too."

"Sure. This is on the king," Andy agreed, reaching for the menu card.

The pink-cheeked waitress came promptly at their signal, waited with praiseworthy patience while Cal Emmett made a momentous decision between a Boston Rhapsody and a Marshmallow Special, and filled the eight orders with care and no assistance whatever. Other girls were offering their aid in spite of the fact that many women sat unserved and indignant.

"Say, this ought to be about enough," Pink suggested, after the third service.

"By golly, the cold's strikin' down to the king's feet," Slim declared, with his mouth full.

Pink frowned and gave another order, uncomfortably aware that here was a situation to be handled with diplomacy. The Happy Family, it would seem, was trying to make him weary of his own joke.

Brother John it was who saved Pink from bankruptcy, and the Happy Family from the hospital. Brother John, most beloved man in all Montana, entered the big room and saw them there, a masculine oasis in a desert of women—which is putting it unchivalrously but truthfully—and came smiling down to them through the crowd. His hand was outstretched, and his face shone with welcome.

The Happy Family liked Brother John. More than once

they had said that Brother John was the only man on earth who could preach to them without hog-tying them first. Their faces lit now at sight of him.

"Hello, Brother John!" they chorused in a way to make the hundred listening women—their number had doubled in the last hour—glance at one another appreciatively. "Come and have some ice cream."

Brother John shook hands all around and called each one by name—by nickname that is—even Big Medicine, the latest addition to the Family, who Brother John had seen but once before in his life, which was one of Brother John's endearing traits. "And how's your Little Doctor and the Old Man? Out for a good time, eh? Well, seeing you're started on the trail of perfect propriety, come on over to our church fair, next door. We're selling pincushions and doilies and telling fortunes to pay for a new bell, and we could use every one of you fellows. Come and help sell pincushions." He chuckled, leaned over the chair of Weary, and whispered mysteriously: "There's a bunch of mighty nice girls over there."

Pink took a rapid survey of their faces. Their general uneasiness made him accept promptly the invitation. He pushed back his chair, gathered up a sheaf of paper checks, and went clanking over to the place that he mentally termed the bar. Happy Jack's defection would, he discovered, cover the bill, but the margin it left was infinitesimal. Fifteen cents, to be explicit.

He turned, waved a signal to his followers, and started for the door. Some of them were anxious to go, a few seemed indifferent now that their first panic had left them, and Cal Emmett, just at the crucial point of bowing to the young lady with three gay feathers in her hat and big, brown eyes which she used to the best advantage—the young lady who had met his glance and smiled twice—Cal Emmett, always ready for a flirtation, refused to budge. Pink waited a moment at the door, and then went buzzing back to him, making more marks for the janitor to swear over.

"Say, yuh mind it means five dollars if yuh don't come," he warned, leaning over Cal's shoulder—and incidentally sending a dimpled smile on his own account in the direction of the blue plumes.

"Not on your life," Cal retorted in a mumbling half whisper. "Yuh call it kingin', but it ain't. It's follow your leader. I used to play it when I was a kid. I wasn't scared to follow yuh in here, was I?"

"Oh, if yuh want to stay five dollars' worth!" grumbled Pink, not quite pleased, and left him.

The girl with the gay feathers rose and picked up her check.

Cal decided suddenly that he ought to obey the mandates of his king, and hurried after Pink, meaning to wait outside the door for the girl.

"Money's just falling into my pocket." Pink was looking down the street after Jack Bates.

"Where yuh going to take us now, King?" Cal asked, with deceitful calm. "Talk about excitement . . . you're a heap more mild than they was in the book. A year-old baby could follow your trail with ease."

"I take notice two of yuh have quit the game already," Pink said sharply.

"Well, we come to town after excitement . . . we. . . ."

The girl with the gay feathers pushed open the door, poised there for a second, and swept past them, a demure smile hiding at the corners of her lips.

Cal did not finish what he was saying. "I owe yuh five, Pink," he announced hurriedly, and went down the street a rod behind the jaunty hat.

"All this suits me fine," Pink remarked, with a rising inflection, and stopped at the store where the church fair was in progress. But Brother John was there before them, his round face smiling in the center of a dozen other faces, mostly of women.

The group broke into fragments when the Happy Family entered and drifted toward the men with welcome written large upon their countenances.

"Oh, you cowboys are just what we want to make our fair a success!" gurgled a large lady, whose skirts crackled when she moved. "We'll give you each a booth . . . and introduce you to some pretty girls who will tell you the prices of things and help you to feel at home. Brother John says you want to help us." She beamed impartially at each in his turn.

"Say, king, here's four dollars and six bits. I'll give yuh the rest tomorrow. I'm goin', by golly!" Slim poured some silver coins into Pink's palm, and went out hastily, slamming the door after himself.

The others stayed, and presently Pink was regretting it very much. The large, crackling lady had heard Slim address him as "king", and straightway led him perforce to a fluttering group and introduced him as "Mister King, the noted cattleman, of whom you have all heard so much, girls . . . the one who just returned from Washington, where he did so much for irrigation in Montana."

Pink thought that she seemed a very well-informed lady, for all her crackling attire, but he wished her information had included the fact that he was not Mr. King. He tried to explain; he blushed adorably, permitted his dimples a brief appearance, and stammered—which was not the way of Pink on his native heath. His explanation got no further than: "I'm afraid I. . . ."

They refused to listen, and they smiled and fluttered

around him and bore him away to a place where there was a huge glass bowl and many little glass cups with handles. In the bowl was something that looked like badly frightened wine, with slices of lemon sailing erratically upon the surface.

"We're going to let you sell the claret punch, Mister King," said a thin young woman with a skinny neck and a kittenish manner. "Just taste it, and see if you do not think it well worth ten cents a drink!" She took a little mug, brushed aside a slice of lemon, dipped gracefully, and held the cup smilingly toward Pink.

Pink had just eaten four elaborate sundaes and made away with two ice-cream sodas and a glass of root beer, but he took the cup, smiled, and said—"Here's looking at yuh."—before it occurred to him that the toast might be considered bad form at a church fair, and drank while the dozen women watched him.

He gave the glass back to the young lady, and said nothing whatever. Indeed, he had no words in his vocabulary to fit claret punch. He felt that as a drink, the less said the better. It might do for women and church fairs, but for a cowpuncher. . . .

He glanced uneasily around the big room, searching for his followers. Big Medicine was apparently quite at his ease, talking with a sweet-faced old lady who sat in a wheel chair. The old lady was listening intently to something he was saying, and she laughed now and then.

Weary and Irish were standing close together, looking so alike that strangers must have been puzzled to tell one from another, and they were laughing and talking to some girls.

He turned disgustedly to see Andy Green, a red-and-yellow turban upon his head and a big-flowered robe wrapped about him, disappearing into a fortune-teller's orange-and-green-striped tent. Andy, with his vivid imagination, thought Pink, would shine as a fortune-teller. And he—*he* must stand there in the middle of the room and sell that off-colored water for ten cents a cup, and call it claret punch, and say it was worth the price.

He couldn't see why he must be gobbled by a lot of old women. In his group, he estimated pessimistically, there wasn't one female under forty. He saw three pretty girls go giggling to get their fortunes told, and the sight made him grit his teeth. A woman to whom he had evidently been introduced as Mr. King came up, bought a cup of punch, and tried to talk as if she knew all about irrigation and Washington and Congress, and then told him how young he was to have done so much for the world. She was just speaking of the responsibilities of one in his position when someone else wanted claret punch.

During the next half hour Pink decided that this was the thirstiest lot of women he had ever seen in his life, which was an erroneous impression born, no doubt, of his nerves.

Once, he bolted unceremoniously during a lull and went over to the orange-and-green tent meaning to get Andy, round up the others, and drift. But Andy was engaged. Behind a curtain made of a couch cover, Pink heard his voice drawling relishfully: "You have an unknown admirer who fell in love with yuh at first sight, and is plumb scared for fear you'll get wise and give him the laugh. He is poor but proud, and he never really knew what love was till he saw yuh. . . ."

"Oh, do tell me what he looks like," murmured a young voice.

"He's tall, and his hair is brown, and his eyes are gray. He. . . ."

Pink turned in great disgust and left the tent. Big Medicine he would have sought next, but Big Medicine was still talking to the sweet-faced old lady. He had quite laid aside his usual blatant complacency, and his face had softened until he was almost good looking in spite of his protruding eyes and his wide mouth.

Pink started toward where he had last seen Weary and Irish. Weary was gravely selling a Dinah doll to a little girl dressed all in white to her very slipper toes, and Irish was absorbed in conversation with two girls.

Pink decided that it was time to go, and clanked back toward the striped tent after Andy. Till that minute, his intent to leave had been largely conditional upon the discomfort of the others. Since they appeared to be enjoying themselves, their king felt that he must try something more distasteful than church fairs. What that something should be he was trying desperately to discover.

Andy was for that moment disengaged. He tripped over his robe in his eagerness to greet Pink when he entered. "Yuh going?" he asked anxiously. "By gracious, another second uh this, and I'd uh been out five plunks." He was unpinning the gaudy robe when Pink stopped him.

"Don't get in a rush," Pink advised calmly. "I just merely looked in to see how you're stacking up. Go on to work . . . here comes a customer." He turned and went out as two girls entered.

Andy refastened his robe, and grinned after the retreating form. "It's working," he murmured, with much satisfaction in his tone.

Outside, Big Medicine saw Pink and signaled hysterically, pointing his thumb over his shoulder toward the door, and raising his eyebrows as high as they would go. Pink shook his head and showed both dimples. He saw Irish and Weary crane necks his way, and reconsidered his decision. He went back to the punch bowl, and dipped ten-cent cups of the fluid with something near to joy in his heart. They were all getting pretty sick of the game—he could see that plainly enough. A little more of it, and they would quit, every mother's son of them. Pink could not think of an easier way to earn twenty dollars. When it was earned, there was still a lot of joy in the town waiting to be collected—and the afternoon was young.

In ten minutes, Irish came buzzing his rowels loudly across the floor, and stopped at Pink's elbow. "Say! How much longer is this thing going to last?" he demanded somewhat aggressively in Pink's ear.

"A lady told me that the fair runs till eleven tonight," Pink replied sweetly. "At six they're going to have a real, honest-to-goodness New England supper . . . baked beans, applesauce, doughnuts, and mince pie. Don't it make yuh hungry?"

"Yes . . . like the devil it does!" retorted Irish, in defiance of the risk he ran of being overheard by the ladies, and stalked back whence he had come, refusing even to taste the claret punch although Pink assured him that it wouldn't cost him anything to try it.

Irish paused a moment beside Weary. "It's all right . . . yuh couldn't pry him loose now with a pickaxe," he whispered in the ear of his double. "Where's the lady?"

It is a mistake to believe that nothing, save orthodox incidents, can happen at a church fair. Certain it is that beneath the smooth surface of punch drinking, doll selling, and subdued chattering made piquant by the presence of five chapped, spurred, and neckerchiefed cowpunchers fresh from the range, an undercurrent of malicious intrigue ran that would have surprised the staid, middle-aged portion of the gathering.

A sprightly woman of frankly admitted thirty-nine approached Pink where he stood for the moment alone. Her first words, murmured for his ears alone, astonished that young man exceedingly. "You poor boy! I saw you standing here looking lonesome, so I just came over to rescue you and keep you company. Mister King, do you know you have perfectly fascinating dimples? Has any girl told you how handsome you are?"

She was a very nice lady, with a husband who she liked very much. She was a friend of the Little Doctor's, and Weary had known her for eight years. Also, Weary had talked very earnestly with her since coming to the fair. But Pink did not know all this. He did not know even that she had a husband. Indeed, she shamelessly led him to believe that she was a lonely female looking for a true soul—a true masculine soul, that is—and she hinted quite openly that Pink appeared to be the man. Within ten minutes, she even went so far as to remind him naïvely that she was not bound by petty conventions concerning what was usually considered the man's privilege.

Some men would have suspected the trick. Some men would have known that the thing was too far-fetched to be possible unless the woman was quite insane. But Pink's abhorrence of feminine adulation quite blinded him to the probability of this. Besides, she was an astute little woman. She made her voice and her eyes carry much of her message.

In fifteen minutes, Pink was in that state of mind which breeds panic. From being a self-poised, mischievous little devil bent upon filching five dollars from each of his fellows without regard to fellowship or the means he employed, he was reduced by one small woman to crimson-faced helplessness. He wanted to go. He actually feared that the little woman was going to ask him outright to marry her. He stuttered —"Excuse me . . . I've got to see. . . ."—and headed for the fortune-teller's tent, which was nearest. He would round up the boys and get out of there, and he hoped that something dreadful would happen to him if ever he invaded another church fair.

But the striped tent was filled—literally packed with women, young and near young. They smiled at him. Pink did not wait to see Andy. He backed out with the same enthusiasm in which he would retreat from a nest of yellow jackets.

He tried Big Medicine, who was not to be found. He went over to the booths where Irish and Weary had been standing. He could see the tips of their heads over the bobbing heads of at least a dozen girls, but he could not get near enough to speak to them, and he could not seem to meet their eyes at all.

"Oh, *here* you are Mister King!" It was the voice of the little woman at his elbow.

Pink started perceptibly, and glared imploringly at the two brown heads ten feet away. The brown heads never so much as turned his way, and the little woman was pulling gently, but very insistently, at his arm.

"If you're tired selling punch," she said sweetly, "we'll just let someone else do it. I know a lovely little corner over there, behind those imitation palms and things. We'll go over there and have a nice long chat, and you can tell me all about your lonely life on the plains, and I'll tell you. . . ."

"Oh, *here* you are, Mister King!" That voice was a big, rollicking one. It belonged to the man who ran a faro bank in a place Pink knew well, and the owner was confronting him with outstretched hand and hypocritically innocent smile.

"Why . . . hello!" Pink articulated, and permitted his hand to be shaken before he backed away.

"Oh, *here* you are, Mister King!" This was another attaché of the place that Pink knew well, and his voice was quite as hearty as the first, his smile as innocent. Again Pink's hand was grasped and shaken.

"Oh, *here* you are, Mister King!" This was the night bartender of the same place. For the third time Pink's limp hand was seized and shaken.

"Oh, *here* you are, Mister King!" This was a man who owned another place which Pink knew well—the place where Irish had first wanted to stop.

Pink's eyes were becoming rather vacant. Someone else bore down upon him, who, Pink was in no condition to say.

"Oh, *here.* . . ." There was absolutely no reason for finishing the greeting. Pink was already at the door. In possibly ten seconds, he was out of sight.

"And here's ten or a dozen of us that never got a chance at him!" said one of the group held in reserve.

The little woman went over to Weary, laughing quietly. Still, it seemed a shame. "He's such a nice boy!" she said remorsefully.

Happy Jack was there, and Jack Bates, and Cal Emmett, and Slim. They were not quite at ease, but in numbers there is composure. They stayed long enough to buy all the dolls for all the little girls, and nearly all the doilies for nearly all the big girls, and to drink all the claret punch—at ten cents a cup. Really it was a splendid day for the church fair.

Then the whole Happy Family—with the exception of Pink—trooped out with their friends, the gamblers and the bartenders and such, and proceeded to collect the joy that was coming to them.

In the purple glow of sunrise, the Happy Family went quietly in a body to the bed tent. Cal Emmett untied the flap and lifted it, with the others crowded close behind him.

"Oh, *here* yuh are, Mister King!" cried Big Medicine.

It took four of them to hold Pink down till his rage cooled.

The White Thread

In November 1906, B. M. Bower was pregnant and due in January—my mother, Della Frances Sinclair, arrived on schedule, but the terrible "Winter of the Blue Snow" had begun early with extreme cold, fierce blizzards, and blue fogs of tiny ice crystals. The bad weather, cabin fever, and Bertha's increasing physical discomfort probably contributed to the somber tone of this dramatic love triangle involving an embittered moody gambler, an innocent young woman, and her raving alcoholic husband as a deadly blizzard approaches. *Everybody's Magazine* rejected the tale as "too bitter". Then it went to editor Charles MacLean. It was so different from Bower's usual style that he held it back over a year. It was published in *The Popular Magazine* in the issue dated February, 1908.

There is a saying that no matter how dark may be the warp and woof of a man's life, if we care enough to look closely, we may be sure of finding somewhere a thread of pure white.

Kirk Haynes was not particularly good to look upon when he rode humped in the saddle, with his hat drawn low over his eyes like the gambler he was, and a certain sardonic twist to his mouth that gave the lie to any suspicion of love for his fellow men. He looked like what he was, a man who lived unto himself, soured and solitary.

When Margaret Johnson met him that morning and looked into his face with big, anxious eyes, her heart sank. But she pulled in her horse and faced him in the brown, frost-hardened trail. Kirk drew rein, also; it was not often that anyone stopped him in the trail—least of all Margaret Johnson. If his eyes changed under the sheltering gray hat brim, she did not notice; certainly his mouth retained its unpleasant twist.

"Kirk," she began, hesitating a bit over the words, "were you out looking, too?"

Kirk observed keenly always; now he saw that her fingers trembled on the bridle reins. "Why should I be out looking? I haven't lost anything," he returned evenly.

Although she tried to read his face, it was all a blank to her. "Kirk, haven't you heard? Don't you know Tom is . . . is lost?"

"So that Methodist preacher said when he saw him drunk in the streets . . . called him 'poor lost brother', if I remember right."

Kirk's tone was smooth, but it was brutal as was apt to be the case when someone stopped him during the long solitary rides he took so often. It was as if he rode far from the habitations of men and resented having his loneliness broken in upon.

The girl winced. "He's lost out here on the prairie somewhere," she explained wistfully. "He's been out two days now. They're looking for him, but they can't get any trace. They were taking him home, and he . . . he went out of his mind and jumped from the wagon and ran. Kirk, I . . . can't you help? You always do things . . . you could find him."

"Thanks, but you're mistaken. The only time I wanted to do anything, I couldn't make good." There was no promise in the cold voice.

Again the girl winced; she understood quite well what it was he meant. Still, her need was great.

"But Kirk, no one could help that. I . . . you wouldn't want

a . . . anybody that cared for someone else. You don't fail very
often. If you really cared, you'd help me find him."

Kirk looked at her sharply. Did women, then, know men
so little? Did they think a man was crazy enough to chase
around over a bleak stretch of prairie looking for the one
human being he hated most of all, to save him? What did she
take him for, he wondered.

"You got a queer way of looking at things," he retorted. "If
I cared, as you say, looks to me like it would be plumb foolish
to go hunting up Tom. And you tell me you cared most for
him . . . which ain't what yuh could call a real strong induce-
ment for me to hunt. You did care, maybe . . . but how about
it now, when he's turned out about as worthless as a man can
get? Do yuh care such a damn' sight *now?*" It was the brute in
him speaking.

She faced him, her eyes hardening. "I do care . . . I always
will care. And you . . . you're worse than all the things they say
about you. I didn't believe any of that before, but I do now.
You haven't any heart or any feelings or any humanity in you.
You're a fiend, Kirk Haynes, and I hate you." She was
shaking with the rage she was in, the rage of pride wounded
by his taunting.

"All right. I'll take your word for all that. It's going to
storm before night, if I'm any judge. You better go find your
Tommy or you're liable to be a widow, you know."

She sat quite still for a minute and looked at him. "It
wouldn't do *you* any good, Kirk Haynes. I hate you!"

"Yuh told me that before," he reminded her calmly. "And
yuh needn't get excited . . . I'm not asking yuh to do anything
else. Go ahead and hate . . . you'll maybe understand some of
what I feel toward your Tommy."

She struck her horse a quick blow and galloped off up the
trail, never once looking back. Kirk sat half turned in the

saddle, his gloved hand resting on the cantle, and watched her go—watched until in the distance she looked merely a black ball rolling away to the skyline—watched until a hollow in the trail hid her from sight. Then he faced to the front, pulled his hat brim a bit farther over his somber blue eyes, and, as he rode on, his clean-shaven lips had more than ever the sardonic twist.

"Women are all the same," he mused bitterly. "And she's like the rest. She takes it for granted I'm a real wolf because I don't love that drunken, low-down cur she married. And she asked me . . . *me* . . . to hunt him up for her. She's a damn' sight better off without him . . . only yuh couldn't beat it into her in a thousand years.

"Women are like that. They go and tie up to some imitation man that ain't capable uh having the care of a dog, because they like the color of his eyes, maybe. *She* took Tommy because his are big and brown . . . like a calf's. And they pass up men that'd kiss the ground they. . . . Hell! Women are sure simple-minded in some ways.

"It's going to storm," he added fretfully to himself. "And the chances are she'll stay out hunting and get caught in a blizzard . . . like as not, she'll get lost. If that precious little sot don't show up, she'll ride the high-lines all winter. And," he repeated with dogged persistence, "she'd be a damn' sight better off without him."

He rode up on a high ridge—leaving the trail to do so —and scanned the surrounding country with eyes that let nothing escape their notice, speculated, with frowning brows, then turned and rode down the ridge on the opposite side, slanting toward the breaks that lay brown and barren away to the southwest.

"Whenever he gets tanked up good and loquacious," he complained to his horse, "he's always discoursing about the

153

time he holed up in the dug-out across the river, and the game he killed, and about that bear he almost got. He always said he'd get that bear, some uh these times. I don't suppose anybody's thought about it . . . not even Margaret. He ought to die . . . it'd be a godsend for *her* . . . only she ain't got the sense to see it."

He got out cigarette material and made a smoke, with the reins held loosely in one hand and his horse walking sedately. He was still frowning morosely. When he had drawn a match along the fork of his saddle and lighted the cigarette, he bent and examined the winding cow trail they were following along a shallow coulée bottom. There was little to see, and he straightened and eyed the sloping walls that shut him away from the rangeland that lay all about.

"The ground's that hard yuh couldn't track an elephant," he grumbled. "And," he repeated for the third time, "it's sure going to storm. Damn a man like Tommy Johnson!"

He went on, heading for the river, yet searching keenly the silent hollows and deep-scarred hills as he rode. He had been ready to go back to the little town when he had met Margaret, back to the place where he dealt faro every night and watched the world—his little world—impassively from the shelter of his hat brim. If he had a friend, he did not know it; he would have told you he did not care. Men treated him with respect and left him alone when they could. His long solitary rides out into the wild by day, his shift at the faro table by night— that was his life, and he preferred to live it alone.

He did not even explain to himself just why he had turned off the trail and ridden back toward the river, or why he cared particularly that the sky threatened snow and wind and cold. His was not the nature that explains, even to itself; what he did was done deliberately, and for the most part silently.

A gray wolf, trotting up a narrow gulch, met him face-to-face and halted in pure astonishment; the traitorous wind had not warned the wolf of an alien presence. But Kirk, although he always carried a gun at his hip, made no move except to smile in more friendly fashion than he would have done had the other been human.

"Hello, old-timer!" he greeted, with cheerfulness in his tone. "Yuh better hike for home . . . if yuh got one. There's weather headed this way that you'll hate to face."

The wolf sniffed inquisitively at the voice, and Kirk pulled his horse close to one wall of the gully, that the wolf might pass. He would have been slow, indeed, to give the trail to a man. With another suspicious sniff the wolf slipped by and darted around a bend. The bounty on wolves was large enough to make them hunted things, rather than hunters; Kirk looked after him and smiled to himself. Then he turned back into the cow trail and went on, his shoulders drooping a bit, his eyes alert and his lips bitter.

He came out upon a little low ridge that sloped gently down to the hurrying, dull gray river. Across, just discernible among the leaf-shorn serviceberry bushes, a sod-roofed cabin peered lonesomely at the water. His range instinct had led him straight to the place he had in mind. Below him a narrow tongue of sandbar reached out from shore. On the extreme point of it, a grotesque figure whirled and shouted.

Kirk stopped and looked attentively down at the man, listening to his insane babbling. His mouth drew into a mirthless grin. "And she's back there scouring the ridges, hunting for . . . *that!*" There was contempt too deep for words in the tone.

"*Right* hand to pardner . . . gran' right 'n' *left!*" Below, the figure swung arms in an imaginary quadrille upon the sandbar. "All-l promenade . . . you know where and I don't care. . . ." Kirk touched heels to his horse and rode down to him.

"Yuh better be thinking uh promenading back where yuh belong," he said, when he was close upon the other. "You're a bird, ain't yuh? Got the whole country out hunting yuh as if yuh was worth saving . . . which, if yuh ask me, yuh ain't."

The dazed brain of the other seemed to recognize an enemy. He glared up at Kirk, then with a yell that held a note of terror, tried to slip past and away, as the wolf had done.

Kirk swung his horse around and checked the other—and in his face was none of the good will with which he had faced the wolf. "No, yuh don't," he remarked grimly. "Yuh stay right where yuh are, damn yuh!"

Tom Johnson, crazed as he was, became animal-like in his desire to flee. He dodged and would have passed on the other side.

"Oh, you're sure a peach of a man!" flared Kirk, and took down his rope. "A locoed horse is good and sensible alongside you." He wheeled to intercept Johnson again, whirled the noose, and smiled sourly when it settled over the shoulders of the crazed man, pinning his arms to his sides.

"Now I guess maybe you'll stand a minute," he said, drawing the rope tightly and holding it while he dismounted. "Oh, yuh scum, yuh need killing! To think they put a bounty on wolves, and let the likes uh you run loose!"

He eyed the man with disgust. Of a truth, Tom Johnson was not just then a pretty sight. He was bareheaded and unwashed. His coat was crusted deep with yellow clay, evidently acquired in drinking from some spring, or perhaps he had fallen before the weather had chilled to freezing. His eyes, big and brown, glared at Kirk with maniacal fury, like the trapped animal he was.

Kirk, advancing watchfully, drew a flask from his pocket and loosened the cork with his teeth. "Throw some of that into yuh, and brace up," he commanded roughly. "Would she care such a lot, I wonder, if she could see yuh now?"

He held the flask to the lips of Johnson, who drank greedily. Still watching closely, he took away the flask when he thought best, and waited till a gleam of reason came into the brown eyes that had stolen from him the love of Margaret.

"Give me some more," pleaded Tom.

Kirk slipped the flask into his pocket and loosened the pinioning noose. "You can have more in a minute," he promised, more impersonally than if he had been speaking to the hills behind him. "Yuh got to brace up and go home. Your . . . they're hunting the hills over to find yuh. It's going to blizzard, and you'll need to be moving." He waited to see if the other grasped his meaning.

"Give me more . . . for God's sake!" Tom tottered forward pitiably.

Kirk brought out the flask again, watched the other swallow great gulps, and snatched it away. "That'll be about enough . . . just now," he decided in the face of the other's insistence. "Did yuh hear me say yuh had to go home?"

"I'll go. I don't know . . . how I got here. I was drunk. I'm a . . . a beast. I know it."

"And that's the truest word yuh ever spoke," cut in Kirk.

"I'll go home. Margaret. . . ."

"You stop right there. If yuh want to live your worthless life out, don't speak that name to *me!*" Kirk spoke with his teeth very close together, so that Tom winced and stepped back a pace.

"Do yuh think," Kirk began again, recovering with some effort the impersonal tone, "yuh could find the way home alone? You'll have to hurry."

Tom looked about him, wonder growing in his eyes which had lost the glare of insanity. "Now, how the devil did I get here?" he asked aloud.

"The point is," Kirk persisted, "can yuh get home alone?"

"Sure. I know where I am. It's twelve miles to town. But I can't savvy how the . . . ?"

"Then get on my horse there, and go. And let me tell yuh, Tom Johnson, yuh better straighten up and be as near human as is in yuh to be . . . or something's liable to happen to yuh. Here, yuh can have one more jolt, and that's got to do yuh till yuh get home."

"But what'll you do? Kirk, I'm no good, but I can't. . . ."

"Damn you, *go!*" In Kirk's fingers the gun he had not used for the wolf backed his authority over the man.

Tom Johnson hesitated but a breath before putting a foot in the stirrup. He knew Kirk Haynes. Still, when he was settled in Kirk's saddle, half-maudlin tears streamed down his cheeks.

"Kirk, you . . . you're a white man . . . I . . . I don't care what they say. I won't forget this. And Margaret. . . ."

"Go, before I *kill* yuh!"

Tom Johnson, snuffling like a whipped boy, went. Went upon Kirk's pet Ace-High, with Kirk's sheepskin-lined sourdough coat buttoned close to his quivering chin.

Kirk, gun in hand to prevent any wavering, watched him go. "And she says she cares for . . . *that!*" he commented, and laughed bitterly to himself.

When the other was out of sight over the hill, Kirk put his gun back and started also. Started afoot, his high-heeled boots making deep dents in the sandbar, his gloved hands thrust into the pockets of his gray sack coat, and his gray hat pulled low over his frowning eyes. He climbed the low ridge, and in a moment he, too, vanished. The sandbar stretching its narrow length into the river had only a jumble of footprints to tell that any had passed that way.

★ ★ ★ ★ ★

The storm came down upon the rangeland, and the gray wolf hurried to his den under a sheltering boulder. The wild range cattle drifted into the deepest coulées they could find, and huddled there before the fury of snow and wind. Tommy Johnson, almost in sight of town, kicked his spurless heels into the flanks of Ace-High and rode with sobered brain and heart sinking. He knew what a blizzard can do when it swoops down upon that open land.

Kirk Haynes, miles back among the breaks, plodded stolidly on in the teeth of it all. Only once he stopped and, in the lee of a cutbank, took off the silk neckerchief he wore, and tied it over his ears. He settled the gray hat firmly, pulling it low as was his way when there was trouble ahead, tied his pocket handkerchief close around his throat, stuffed his chilled fingers back into his pockets, and left the scant shelter of the bank to struggle on.

Gray afternoon changed to grayer night, when all objects were hidden and he had only instinct for guide. The town, he knew, lay off there whence came the snow and wind, so into the snow and wind he burrowed doggedly.

"Wonder if the damn' coyote got home all right," he muttered once.

He was not thinking of the wolf, but of the man. Thinking, too, of Ace-High, and wondering if Tommy Johnson would know enough to blanket him well and feed him. Ace-High was about the only friend Kirk felt that he could justly claim for his own.

"Wonder if she had sense enough to get in out uh this white hell."

He was climbing wearily a slippery ridge then. On top, he halted a minute to breathe, and it seemed to him that both snow and wind came down from all quarters upon him. He

159

stopped and stood, waiting to see from which direction they really came, waited a shade too long. When he started on, the way he took led not to town, but farther into the wild.

More hills he climbed, and some sent him sliding down into deep coulées where the whirl of powdery snow was confusing to all senses alike. Times there were when he must stop and hunch together, his face hidden in his chilled hands that he might breathe. Times when frightened cattle lumbered out of his uncertain path, and lowed wistfully after his retreating form.

"Wish I knew where that wolf hangs out," he told himself wearily. "I'd go bunk with him tonight . . . I'll gamble he'd take a fellow in and be sociable. Maybe he'd give me a bone to gnaw on, and that wouldn't be so worse, either."

Under a shelving bank he stopped to get a breath free of snow flour. Even here it swirled spitefully in upon him as if to warn him that it knew exactly where he was, and could not be foiled in so simple a fashion. He was very, very tired. He looked dully out into the whirl he could not see, and listened to the faint, sinister swishing of the storm.

"He had oceans uh time to get home," he muttered. "Ace-High was good for it at his old gait . . . and he'd take the damn' little pinhead to town without any guiding. And that whisky ought to keep him straight for that length uh time. Oh, I guess he made it all right."

He got out his smoking material and huddled close against the bank, managed to light a cigarette although his fingers were like dried twigs. He smoked and gazed out at nothing, while the snow swirled in upon him. The cigarette burned down to his lips, but he could not make another. His fingers were too useless, and he was too tired. In a minute, though, he would go on; he ought to get out of the breaks and on to the level pretty soon now. He slipped down until he was half sitting, half lying in the snow, with the clay bank at his back. It was a lot warmer under the bank where the wind couldn't cut through him. If he had a blanket, he thought, he could spend the night there quite comfortably.

I've got to get busy, though, he meditated languidly. *If I just had my sourdough coat . . . but he couldn't have made out without it. He would sure have cashed in quick when this here Klondike Chinook struck if I hadn't found him.* Oh, well, he summed the matter up drowsily, *if it's as she says, if she likes him and wants him, I guess she's entitled to have him, but she's sure got queer taste. It's getting a lot warmer. I'll have to be moving . . . pretty soon.*

The snow swirled in and found only a tall figure stretched quietly in the shelter of the bank—asleep. It sifted down noiselessly, while the fury of the blizzard hurled past and went shrieking up the narrow coulées. Still the snow sifted in and over him. When morning broke, a smooth blanket of pure white, tucked close by fingers unseen, covered a long, low something under the clay bank.

The Western Tone

Although like most writers, B. M. Bower appropriated whatever was useful from real life, she was never guilty of blatant exaggeration and exploitation. Her opinion of writers who employed such tactics is clear in this wickedly witty portrayal of a literate, intelligent cowboy's outraged reaction to "local color" gone awry. He kidnaps the unethical, greedy, and extremely gullible author with an irresistible lure, and administers a heavy dose of clever but relatively harmless revenge—except to the writer's naïveté and ego. The cowboy does not understand magazine deadlines or editors' contempt for readers' intelligence, so his revenge is not complete, but the writer will never forget his "cure". The story first appeared in the March, 1908 issue of *The Popular Magazine*.

High Note stretched himself lazily, and reached for his tobacco sack on the coffee-box table beside his bunk. "What yuh readin', Kid?" he asked in the tone of one who doesn't care whether or not he is answered.

Kid looked up briefly from last month's *Illustrated Magazine*. "A peach of a story, High Note, and the hero's a dead ringer for you. He's called Upper C, I take notice. And he wears a robin's egg blue neckerchief, smokes cigarettes, and says damn, and drinks and gambles habitual. If that ain't your brand. . . ."

"Lemme see it a minute." High Note held the match a second longer to his cigarette, got a good puff or two, and reached for the magazine. Kid held it a bit farther off. "Aw, wait till I finish reading about the girl," he protested. "She's got black eyes, and. . . ."

"Hell! Hand it over here." When High Note adopted just that tone, it was better to grant any little request he made. Kid surrendered the magazine reluctantly. High Note turned back to the beginning and began to read, curiously at first, then incredulously and with the anger growing in him. It was as Kid had said: the hero did certainly seem to be a fairly accurate portrayal of High Note himself, and it never occurred to him to feel flattered at the resemblance.

"Listen at this once," he said after reading a few minutes in silence with frowning eyebrows. " 'Upper C, his flopping gray hat tilted back from his sun-bronzed, immobile features, galloped into the evanescent effulgence of the mauve and gold and deep crimson sunset.' Now, what the devil"—he glared at Kid—"do they mean by that? I never galloped into no such ungodly sunset in my life . . . not even when I was full to the guards uh red-eye. And any man that calls my features immobile had better pack a gun when he ambles across my trail, because I'll sure make him a heap uh trouble when I meet up with him."

"Aw, that's mild . . . wait till yuh get to the girl!" tittered Kid.

High Note read further, snorting with the regularity of punctuation marks. "Look at this here . . . 'His brooding eyes turned often to where day was dying in a welter of purples and reds!' I've heard uh setting hens being broody, but damn if I ever was like that."

"You wait," Kid admonished again. "You'll go straight in the air when yuh get t' where. . . ."

"Hell! 'Upper C, swinging his long spur-tipped legs backward, leaned in the saddle and rode like an Indian.' Damn it, is my legs spur-tipped? And if so, how'd it happen?" He cast the magazine far from him. "And I may be a no-account cuss . . . I won't deny but what my virtues ain't always on the surface while my faults loom up prominent . . . but damn if I ever rode like an Injun!" There was more that he said upon the subject, but it was not meant for repetition.

Kid went over and picked up the magazine and smoothed the crumpled leaves. He found the place where High Note had been reading, and brought it back to him.

"Aw, go ahead and read the rest," he begged insinuatingly. "I want to see what yuh think uh the girl part. She's got black eyes, and rides a red roan, and her hair curls around her ears. And you 'n' her is plumb gone on each other, and then a fellow comes along and tries to butt into the game, and you go after him with a six-gun . . . that's when yuh galloped into the sunset . . . and yuh find him, where his horse has fell on him. . . ."

"Saw off!" commanded High Note in a peculiar grating tone. "You're lying, Kid, and it ain't safe to pick your subjects so careless. There ain't a man living that would dare to write up. . . ."

"Well, darn it all, yuh don't have to believe what I'm telling yuh, if yuh don't want to. Read it yourself, darn yuh."

High Note—which, of course, was only a name bestowed upon him by his fellows—took a long, disconcerting look at Kid before he let his fingers close over the offending magazine. Sometimes Kid was not above elaborate joking, and he did not always choose his subjects with tact. But from the look of him, Kid was not joking now. Besides, even he would hardly dare joke upon a theme that men did not even mention in the presence of High Note. Kid was foolish and unthinking, but he valued his health and had no particular reason to court suicide.

So High Note, taking these things into consideration, took the magazine and read deliberately to the end of the story, the end that painted with redundant, high-sounding sentiment the final renunciation of Upper C, and told how he had blessed the girl with black eyes, asked her plaintively to remember him sometimes, and had ridden away into the gloom, leaving his love, presumably, to his rival whose life he had saved.

It was all according to the popular style of fiction, and quite up to the accepted standard of Western stories, but High Note, when he read the last paragraph, grated his teeth unpleasantly. Galloping into an unusual sunset was nothing to this; even the assertion that he had ridden like an Indian he might have overlooked. But to have him get cold feet just at the critical point of his game—the artistic viewpoint was utterly lost upon High Note—made his heart rage.

Up to that point it had been true enough. High Note was in love with a black-eyed girl—a girl who rode a red-roan horse. He had been annoyed by a rival, had started out just as the story read—barring galloping into that particular sunset, which High Note would never admit doing—to hunt up his rival and, in the words of High Note, drag it out of him proper. He had found the rival lying where his horse had fallen on him and was still resting resignedly—and it was here that the story waved flippant *adieu* to truth and went careening off into sentiment.

In the story, Upper C had come upon the rival at a critical moment, just when a band of wild cattle were pawing and bellowing about the man, working up their appetites and their enthusiasm. "In another moment"—according to the story—"they would have been upon him. Already the hot breath of the leader was bathing his ashen face in a fetid steam. Upper C, yelling like an Apache, emptied his revolver full in the face of the blood-maddened leader. It was too much. . . ."

Truly, it was too much. The plain truth was that High Note had helped the fellow on his horse—there being no ravenous wild cattle threatening to devour him—and had taken him over to the hotelkeeper, not, as fiction had it, to the house of the black-eyed girl, where she was to nurse him back to life and health.

He had left the rival with the injunction to remember that, when that leg of his got all right, High Note would see him again, and that he would come shooting. He had not, as had been told, spouted long, well-rounded sentences of renunciation to the girl, and ridden away into the gloom to efface himself and make feminine readers weep. That was pure invention on the part of the perpetrator of the yarn, and it hurt the pride of High Note beyond words.

He had not effaced himself, and he had no intentions of doing so. He had wanted a reasonable time for the healing of the rival's injuries, and then had taken much trouble to find him and renew hostilities. The only reason his vengeance was still unsatisfied was that the rival had recovered sooner than High Note had anticipated, and had gone away somewhere.

High Note, in possession of the battlefield, was still hoping to make the girl say yes to the question he wanted answered that way. She was perverse, of course, and had so far persisted in saying the wrong word or no word at all. But High Note was what his fellows would call a stayer, and so he still had hopes.

"Kid," he said, turning down a corner of the leaf where the story began, and smoothing the rumpled pages of the magazine, "I'd give a lot to know who it was wrote this tale. Whoever done it, it's a cinch he meant me . . . and, meaning me, I guess I got a right to get into the game."

"Sure he meant you." Kid grinned sympathetically. "And

I bet I can point yuh out the gazabo that's guilty. Yuh mind that fellow they called Meadowlark, that was stopping at the home ranch last summer . . . the fellow with the gold mine in his front teeth? I'll betcher what yuh like, it was him. I know he had a typewriter at the ranch, and he done a lot uh chasing after his mail. It was him, all right." Kid leaned back to study the effect of this information. Then he added carelessly: "Billy Burns told me he's back there again . . . come out on the stage Tuesday." Kid Burke loved trouble—when he was not personally concerned in it.

High Note sat for long minutes saying nothing, although his actions were eloquent of the mood he was in. First he took down his gun from the peg where it hung in its scabbard, toyed with it thoughtfully, emptied the cylinder and inspected the cartridges, then slipped them carefully back into place. Kid Burke watched him with keen interest. High Note had never stained his hands with murder, but he was quite capable of giving his detractors some uneasy moments, and had even been known to lodge a bit of lead where it was not particularly dangerous for lead to be. His enemies and detractors, therefore, were a bit shy of High Note when his temper went bad.

He laid the gun down after a while, and took up the magazine, going methodically through the story again from beginning to libelous end. This time he made no comment whatever during the reading; he seemed absorbed in the effort to weigh each sentence carefully and separately.

"Kid," he said grimly, when he was through, "I guess we'll ride over to the ranch tomorrow. I want to meet up with that Meadowlark."

Kid grinned appreciatively, but wisely said nothing. He began taking off his boots, still smiling in anticipation of the morrow.

Fate might have been kinder than it was to Albert Meadowcroft Rogers; it might have broken High Note's leg or arm or something, and so prevented their meeting. As it was, High Note galloped up to the corral of the home ranch and met Albert Meadowcroft Rogers face-to-face. Albert was out roosting on a rail, taking notes, while a cowpuncher rode a buckskin horse spectacularly in the corral. Albert was fitting phrases to the revolutions of the buckskin, so that, when he put a pitching horse into one of his popular Western stories, the description would be thrillingly convincing to his editors —the public didn't matter so much.

High Note dismounted and clanked over to roost beside Albert. "Hello, Meadowlark," he greeted amicably. "Rounding up stuffing for another story?"

Albert looked at High Note apprehensively, and smiled a faint greeting. He also blushed a bit. It is embarrassing to meet one's characters face-to-face like that, and to have a suspicion that the character knows what you have been doing with him in print.

"That is a great yarn yuh got in the *Ill-ustrated*," High Note went on, rolling himself a cigarette. "At least, I took it to be yours. And I'd like to ask, out uh curiosity, was yuh thinking uh me when you mixed that tale?"

"Why . . . what makes you think so?" queried Albert, blushing the more and wetting his pencil nervously. "I'm sure. . . ."

"Oh, it's vanity, maybe, but it ain't every bone-headed cowpuncher gets wrote into a romance like that. I just thought some uh the scenes an' incidents looked darn' familiar, and Upper C . . . well, I ain't no musical prodigee, but it looked like ringing a change on High Note, which is the name I answer to when the tone is polite and friendly. Maybe

I ain't been put into no romance for an admiring world to read."

"Oh, well . . . if you consider it an honor. That is, a story isn't supposed to be fact. And . . . by Jove! Did you see that?"

High Note turned his eyes briefly to the gyrations of the buckskin, and then frowned a warning at Kid Burke, who was plainly looking for the battle to begin. "What I'd like to know," he said with friendly persistence, "is did you write that tale?"

"Oh, I wrote it," admitted Albert with easy indifference. "I write stories of the West, you know, but you mustn't think. . . ."

"That's all right. I ain't thinking anything I ain't got the papers for," High Note put in humbly. "It must be great to make up a story like that, and have it sound so damn' real a fellow thinks sure he's it."

Albert shook his head and smiled disparagement of the praise. Then he turned the subject diplomatically to the horse and its disheveled rider. "I only wish I could have brought an artist out with me," he said. "Look there! That would make a corking picture . . . all you fellows are deuced picturesque, you know."

"The hell yuh say!" High Note looked inordinately pleased. "Yuh know, I'd 'a' gone plugging along all my life and never savvied that we was anything but just common folks."

"Look at that fellow . . . Broncho Bill . . . he's a character worthy a place. . . ."

High Note pinched out his cigarette stub, and grunted disdain. "Yuh think so, because yuh just stick here at the ranch and don't see what's really worth your time. Down at our line camp, now. . . ."

"Is it . . . er . . . picturesque . . . more so than this?" Albert turned his pale eyes eagerly toward the other.

"Is it?" High Note snorted with mirth. "Well, say. You come down and stop with Kid and me a few days, and I'll gamble you'll have the damnedest, pictureskest time uh your life. If yuh want the real thing. . . ."

"I do," Albert averred. "I've taken a lot of trouble to come out here and get into the middle of things. What I'm after is the real Western tone, the. . . ."

"And I'm the man that can sure put yuh next," enthused High Note. "You come on with us . . . you'll sure be in the middle uh things down to our line camp. And if Western tone is what yuh want, why we've got it to throw to the birds."

"You're awfully good," beamed the guileless Albert Meadowcroft Rogers, while visions of stories that would "take" and checks large in proportion danced gleefully in the background of his literary mind. "I'll go. And I don't mind telling you now, you know, that you are one of the most picturesque characters I've met out here, and maybe that fellow, Upper C, was modeled after you a bit."

"You don't say." High Note grinned, climbing limberly down from his lofty perch. "Well, I figure that I owe you something for that great honor, so you come along with me and I'll sure make it right."

Albert Meadowcroft Rogers, like the fool he was, went.

Two miles out from the ranch High Note suddenly remembered that he had forgotten something, and turned back, leaving Albert to go on with Kid Burke, who was near bursting with curiosity and disappointment. He had expected, and with reason, that something would happen when those two got together, and instead they seemed the best of friends.

When High Note reached camp forty minutes or so behind them, he looked fagged and thankful to be rid of his burden which was Albert's typewriter, one of those large, heavy things, mighty awkward to carry on horseback, especially when the horse does not take kindly to strange objects in the hands of its rider.

"I thought yuh might need it," High Note explained to the astonished owner of the machine.

"Er . . . ye-es . . . but if I did, I couldn't do anything without paper and carbon."

"Hell!" said High Note, staring blankly.

"Oh, it doesn't matter in the least. I only mean to stay a day or two, and I probably shall not do anything more than take a few notes. Of course," he added politely, "it was awfully thoughtful of you, and I won't forget your kindness in thinking of it."

"Oh, I'm going to be a heap more kinder than that." High Note grinned. "I'm going to haze Kid back to the ranch after the paper and carbonic acid, so yuh can get to work right after supper."

"Carbon," corrected Albert politely. "It's a kind of paper to make copies. But really, you mustn't bother . . . I assure you I shall not need it at all."

"Oh, yuh might . . . there ain't any telling," persisted High Note. "Kid, you saddle up a fresh horse and hike back and bring our friend's paper and carbolic, immediate. And fetch some envelopes. We ain't got a damn' one in the shack."

Albert protested, but there was a look in the eyes of High Note that sent Kid hurrying to obey. He couldn't understand High Note, but he was of a hopeful nature, and he went willingly.

It was not until after Kid was back with the paper and envelopes, and the supper dishes were washed, that the elaborate friendliness of High Note changed. He placed the typewriter on the table, put the bundle of paper beside it, trimmed the two little horns off the lamp wick so that the chimney ceased accumulating smoke, pushed the lamp close to the typewriter, and pulled a soapbox up to the table.

After that he took his gun out of its scabbard on the peg at the head of his bunk, got the magazine that had in it the story of Upper C, and motioned Albert Meadowcroft Rogers to be seated on the soapbox.

"This here romance yuh wrote up about me," High Note began, in the tone which Kid Burke recognized as heralding things, "needs a lot uh fixing. And I'm here to see that the fixing is done, and done proper. Get busy with that writing animal, and write it over the way I tell yuh."

The eyes of Albert protruded noticeably. He hesitated, and eyed High Note dubiously, until High Note took to fingering his gun in a way to make one's nerves crumple. Whereupon Albert went over and sat down on the soapbox.

"Get busy," ordered High Note. "Start her going . . . you know how I mean. Write down the name just as she stands here, and start her off. I'll stop yuh when yuh get to that there sunset, which I won't stand for a holy minute."

Albert gathered some inkling of High Note's meaning, and grasped feebly at his courage. "I can write it over, if you insist," he said, "but what good will it do? It's in print the other way, and I. . . ."

"And she's going to be in print the right way, before another month rolls around, or things'll happen," High Note cut in, a trace of temper showing in his voice. "Yuh need killing, for taking a law-abiding citizen and writing up things he's done that ain't nobody's business but his own. Why, damn yuh, yuh ought to be hung for bringing me and the girl before the public that way, when we ain't done anything to deserve it. I'd 'a' sure shot yuh up some for that, only yuh didn't tell the thing straight, and so I've got to keep yuh whole till yuh square things. There's a lot uh things in this story that don't go. Now, get busy!"

Albert Meadowcroft Rogers cast one terrified look at High Note, and rolled some paper into the machine. Then he began to expostulate. It was no use, he said. The story had already appeared in print, and it could not be used again. As for having it in the magazine inside a month, he asserted tremblingly, the thing was impossible—utterly impossible.

High Note smile unpleasantly. "If yuh swallow all yuh hear," he said, unmoved by the argument, "there's a lot uh things that's utterly impossible. But my high and wide experience with men goes to prove that there's mighty few things that can't be did . . . when yuh got a good six-gun to back your requests. You ask Kid, here, what he'd do in your place, right now."

"Knowing High Note a lot, I couldn't get busy a darn' bit too soon," testified Kid, without waiting to be asked. Then he grinned; Kid Burke was beginning to enjoy himself very much.

Albert Meadowcroft Rogers, looking unhappily from one to the other, for once decided wisely. He got to work writing, as High Note, magazine in hand and gun within easy grasping distance, revised and dictated. When he came to the place where "Upper C, swinging his long, spur-tipped legs backward, leaned in the saddle and rode like an Indian," he really feared that High Note would murder him without waiting to finish the story. But at the worst he had only to listen shiveringly while High Note gave his sincere and profane opinion of the man who would write such stuff about white folks.

Then the work proceeded tumultuously. Since Albert was extremely nervous and not an expert typist at best, he made frequent and horrifying blunders in his copy, and, since High Note took each page as it left the machine and went over it

173

carefully and mercilessly, making no allowance for the state of Albert's nerves, there were intervals when the most seasoned storyteller would be obliged to draw the traditional veil.

The hours dragged to midnight, and during the quieter moments, when High Note dictated and Albert clicked out the sentences more or less correctly on the machine, Kid Burke nodded sleepily. He would not go to bed, for he expected things of High Note when the story reached that point where Upper C rescues his rival from the band of bloodthirsty range cattle. From there on, even Kid hesitated to prophesy what might happen to Albert.

As a matter of fact, however, nothing much happened. Kid woke once to hear High Note calling the literary young man some very startling names, and to see Albert cowering on the soapbox and trying, seemingly, to hide behind his typewriter while he stared glassily at the big murderous-looking revolver that almost touched the fingers of High Note. Kid sat up and blinked his eyes open, but High Note was merely giving Albert some much-needed information about the habits and tastes of range cattle, so that Kid went back to snoring.

When he woke again, the sun was shining in at the window. Evidently Albert and High Note had made a night of it. They were not quite through, even yet, for High Note was finding fault with a letter that Albert had written, at his behest, to the editor of the *Illustrated*. The general tone, it seemed to High Note, was altogether too apologetic.

"And it won't go, savvy?" he was saying. "You can frame up a better letter than that, and the sooner yuh get at it, the better appetite you'll have for breakfast. Why didn't yuh put in what I told yuh to? That you wanted this tale printed in the May number of the *Illustrated*, or things would be popping around his vicinity. Why didn't yuh tell it had to be did? Now, get busy . . . and see to it that yuh don't have to frame up a third letter, because it's liable to be unpleasant for yuh around here."

Albert Meadowcroft Rogers looked as if it were already sufficiently unpleasant for him. His face was pasty white, and his hair much rumpled, and there were wide purple rings under his pale eyes. When he lifted his hand from the keyboard to roll in a fresh sheet of paper, his fingers shook so that he could scarcely accomplish even that simple task.

The third letter was as High Note wished it to be, although to Albert it was like being compelled to commit suicide to write in that way; the editor of the *Illustrated* might not kill him, but he certainly would never buy another of his stories. He decided that he would privately write a letter to the editor, explaining in full the situation and his own deadly danger. And then he wondered if this horrible fellow with the unpleasantly piercing eyes and the robin's egg-blue neckerchief and the six-shooter was a mind-reader, for High Note killed his hopes in one matter-of-fact sentence.

"You'll camp right here with Kid and me, Meadowlark," he said, folding the letter and putting it in the big envelope with the revised version of Upper C's adventure. "Kid'll take this to town and mail it right after breakfast, and you'll stay with me till an answer comes. Maybe I'm some suspicious, but I ain't a fool. Yuh ain't going to have any chance to queer the game on the quiet . . . savvy? All correspondence with the affeety East stops right where she is till this romance is in print proper. And if anybody shows up from the home ranch and wants to know how yuh like living down here in a line camp, remember, yuh like it fine. You're so stuck on batching with Kid and me that you're liable to stay quite a spell. Kid'll give us some chuck in a minute, and then yuh can roll in and pound your ear for a few hours . . . yuh look like yuh need it, all right."

Albert Meadowcroft Rogers shivered a little. He did not know why he should be made to pound his ear. It sounded unpleasant. However, he made no comment. He had learned during those long night hours the value of silence and the futility of argument. The prospect of chuck, even though Kid Burke was counted a good cook, did not appeal to him. With High Note and his gun sitting opposite, he could scarcely choke down a half cup of coffee, and, as for eating, it was out of the question, even though High Note commanded him to stake himself to a full plate.

After breakfast he discovered one thing that cheered him a bit. High Note announced to Kid that he also was "going to pound his ear", and that Kid was to wake him when he got ready to start for town. So Albert gathered that the ominous phrase merely meant sleeping. At another time he would have reached for his notebook to jot down so picturesque a term, but now he had no heart for it. He felt as if he never wanted to see or hear anything picturesque and Western again as long as he lived. He lay down on Kid's bunk, and, because Nature does sometimes take things into her own hands, he straightway fell asleep in spite of the fact that he still had suspicions of High Note and his gun.

So began Albert Meadowcroft Rogers's sojourn at the line camp of the T-Down—a sojourn that savored strongly of captivity. To be sure, neither of the men offered him bodily injury of any sort, but there was always a chance that they might. High Note wore his gun and belt even when playing a peaceful game of seven-up with Kid at night, and he would relate fearsome tales of shootings he had been in, and men who had crossed his rope and had been laid away in some lonely hollow to wait for other and higher judgment than his.

"And you can gamble, Meadowlark," he would often finish, "when a man goes up against a real 'puncher and tries any funny business, that man is dead certain to get all that's coming to him. A fellow may toy with him a while, and let him run on the rope a few times just for amusement . . . but he sure ain't going to escape the just and horrible end that's framed up for him. Um-m-m! About how long did yuh say it would take to hear from that jasper we sent the story to?"

Then Albert would moisten his lips and give the necessary information, always reminding High Note nervously that there is ever a chance of delayed mails to be reckoned with, so that one can never tell exactly when a letter would reach any given point.

High Note would say "unh-huh" in a tone that told nothing, and would finger his six-shooter absently, and Albert would take a fit of shivering. He planned escape of nights and, by day, saw that there was nothing but certain death in the attempt. High Note always turned loose the gentle old cow pony that Albert had ridden from the ranch, and never caught him up except when Albert was invited, mildly and ironically, to go with them on all the rides which came in a day's duty. Albert went, because High Note always wore the gun and had that glint in his eyes that makes one hurry to grant any and all requests. But Albert went a prisoner, and he did not enjoy the excursions.

Whenever they came upon a particularly uncanny spot in the rough surrounding country, that spot always had a gruesome history attached to it. High Note would relate the history in all its horrible details. Albert would listen reluctantly and with eyes protruding. Kid Burke, on such occasions, would drop behind and omit occasional gurgles—presumably of horror—and, when High Note was through, he would turn to Albert and say gravely: "Now there's Western tone to burn, Meadowlark. Soon as yuh get back to the shack, yuh better get out the writing machine and write her up. You can gamble on its being straight goods, all right."

Albert would smile painfully; the mere thought of a story or a typewriter gave him a sick feeling in his stomach.

So passed twelve days of misery such as Albert had never dreamed would come to him. There was one day when Broncho Bill rode up to the camp and stopped for dinner. Albert was in an agony to let Broncho know the plight he was in, and to ask for deliverance from the delayed vengeance of High Note. But High Note was there with the gun, and there was no chance for a word. When Broncho Bill asked Albert how he liked camping, Albert opened his lips to tell his woe. But High Note glanced at him just then, so Albert swallowed twice, and said—"Fine."—weakly and without enthusiasm.

"You bet!" High Note added cheerfully. "Meadowlark is having the time of his life, all right. He goes every place we go, and is absorbing enough Western tone to last him . . . as long as he's going to need it." The last part of the sentence may have sounded ambiguous to Broncho Bill, but Albert understood and turned pale.

"What yuh packing your gun for, High Note?" Broncho asked curiously. High Note, whose day it was to get the meals, was stooping over the stove turning slices of bacon. "Afraid that hog-meat is going to come alive and tackle yuh?"

High Note straightened, and pulled the gun a bit forward. "Oh, I wear it to please Meadowlark," he said calmly. "He sure loves to see Kid and me togged up good and picturesque. He says I'm the most pictureskest character he's ever went up against."

Albert Meadowcroft Rogers walked unsteadily to the door and stood leaning a bit heavily against the casing while he gazed dim-eyed at the jagged bluff opposite. What he thought no man may know.

The fateful day came when Kid Burke, returning from town, brought a long envelope with the address of *The Illustrated Magazine* in one corner. Albert took it with shaking knees and trembling fingers. His reprieve was ended, and the worst was about to come upon him. Albert had served his literary apprenticeship; he knew a rejected story when he saw it.

High Note received the news in a silence more terrible than the highest flight of profane eloquence. Not even when he read the scathing letter from the editor to Albert did his mask-like countenance change. He folded letter and manuscript again, pushed them back into the envelope, and weighed it a moment on his pink palm. Then he lifted his eyes and took a long and disconcerting look at Albert's ashen face.

"Well," he said slowly, while Albert was thinking that in another minute he should go raving mad, "she didn't go through. It'd uh been a heap better for you, Meadowlark, if the fellow had took this tale. Yuh can't go and tell the angels I never give yuh a chance to square yourself. And when yuh get there, yuh want to impress it on their minds that I don't hold myself noways responsible for your being with 'em. In your misguided zeal for Western tone and picturesqueness, yuh brought it on yourself. I hope yuh make this plain to 'em, Meadowlark."

After that he became perfectly silent and spoke no other word to his victim. He ejected the cartridges from his gun, cleaned and oiled the weapon very painstakingly, and put in fresh shells from his belt. Albert, watching him fascinated, ate no supper that night. Instead, he went to his bunk and lay turned to the wall.

When Kid Burke opened his reluctant eyes at dawn, the first thing they saw was a tumbled heap of bedding in the bunk Albert had occupied. Kid got up and passed his hands quickly over the empty blankets—and found them quite cold. He went to the door, looked toward the corral, and snickered to himself when he saw that no horse was missing, snickered because the home ranch was a long fifteen miles away, and bad walking at that. He went back and laid ungentle hands upon High Note. "Wake up!" he bellowed into High Note's ear. "That tame Meadowlark uh yours has flown."

High Note knuckled his eyes and sat up. "Are we shy a horse?" he asked, when he was sufficiently awake to grasp the news.

"Nope. He walked."

The two looked at each other for a minute, and then laughed softly.

"We've got the typewriter to remember him by," said Kid, and added: "It's a cinch he never comes after it."

High Note grinned, and reached for his cigarette material. "I'll bet yuh a new saddle," he offered, "that he don't ramble around on this range no more, hankering after Western tone and a-lookin' for picturesque characters to put into his darned romances."

Albert Meadowcroft Rogers never did.

Hawkins

This story in the Lady Slipper series continued Bower's shift away from humor. It was published in *The Popular Magazine* (11/15/19). Brant Whipple returns recuperated from the stampede accident with a new friend. H. H. Holt, a recent hire, cautiously renews acquaintance with the newcomer. Suspicion that the two share an unsavory past grows in a bad-tempered hand. Suddenly fast action erupts into a shocking conclusion. Bower's LONESOME LAND, an autobiographical novel, explored similar themes—abuse, betrayal, sacrifice, and defiance of law and convention for the sake of higher principles—and became Little, Brown's first B. M. Bower book, issued in February, 1912. By October 1st the book had sold out ten printings.

Bleached a sallow white from lying long upon his back in a hospital, scarred from the hurts which took him there, and smiling once more to sit in leather and feel a real horse between his legs, Brant Whipple rode slowly up to the camp of the Lady Slipper and yelled—"Hello!"—in a voice to include even the horse wrangler watching his herd a furlong away.

Lockie, the foreman, stuck his head out from under the flaps of the cook tent and answered the greeting guardedly, as if he were consciously refraining from any enthusiasm over the return of the absent one. He saw that Brant was not alone, and came out of the tent and up to the riders. Other members of the outfit were appearing from diverse places and were welcoming Brant while they eyed the stranger.

Brant caught sight of the foreman and instinctively sat more erect in the saddle. "Say, Lockie," he began with an assumption of ease which he perhaps did not feel, "when I left, you was working short-handed . . . I thought maybe you'd be able to put my friend here to work. He's a 'puncher I met up with while I was laying around with the hospital bunch, working the wobble outta my legs and waiting for the doctor to turn me loose. Can yuh make use of him? Hawkins, this is Lockie McNab, wagon boss of the Lady Slipper."

The two men recognized the introduction with a nod, and Lockie looked the other over with no pretense at disguising the inspection; when he answered Brant's question, his tone was noncommittal, for he did not believe it politic to encourage his men in bringing him every unknown idler who they might chance to meet.

"I just took a man on a week or two ago," he said, and glanced toward Three H, bulking large in the shadow of the bed wagon.

Brant's face plainly showed his disappointment as he turned to Hawkins. "Well, there's other outfits using lots uh men," he began, when Lockie spoke again, this time to the stranger.

"If you can *ride,*" he qualified, "maybe I can find a place for yuh. Can you handle the rough string?"

Hawkins gave his slim body a twist and flicked a high weed off to his right with his quirt. "I can tell yuh better when I see how rough it is," he retorted carelessly. "But I'm willing to try it a whirl, anyhow."

That was reasonable and unassuming and smacked of a complete understanding of the business, for none but the novice will promise largely where strange horses are concerned —horses qualified to membership in the rough string, that is.

Lockie studied him more attentively and more favorably.

His eyes went to the horse and rested there covetously.

"That your horse?" he asked irrelevantly, going closer.

"It sure is," replied Hawkins quickly, as he laid a hand upon the arched neck where the light gave a sheen of pure copper.

"Pretty good-looking animal," Lockie paid grudging tribute.

"Say," Brant cut in with enthusiasm, "yuh ought to see him in action if yuh want a pretty sight! I'll bet that same *caballo* can get out and do his seventy-five miles and come into camp stepping high and handsome. Ain't that right?" He appealed to Hawkins.

Hawkins smoothed the shiny neck with a touch that was worshipful. "Yes . . . or a hundred, if he had to," he boasted. "I rode him eighty between dark and dawn once," he added with a certain hesitation in his tone, and bit his lip immediately afterward, as if he regretted the assertion which might be received with incredulity.

"And gentle!" Brant went on admiringly. "Why Hawkins can crawl all around him . . . between his front legs and out between his hind hoofs, and him never moving. Why, a baby could play under him."

"Yes," Hawkins assented modestly, "he's sure gentle enough."

Bill came up and stroked the horse upon the nose and got a dainty lip nibble in return. "What's his name?" he asked, grinning his pleasure.

"I call him Bird." Hawkins turned then to Lockie. "Well, do I get on?"

"If you want to tackle the rough string . . . but I may as well tell you it ain't smooth riding!"

Hawkins smiled as he swung down from the saddle. "I dunno as I ever saw a rough string that was," he observed, although he knew well enough what Lockie meant. "Come, Bird," he invited caressingly, and started afoot for the rope corral.

The horse, picking his way daintily among the tin cans that the cook had thrown out, followed closely behind him and nibbled now and then at his master's hat brim with his lips.

Brant, content to ride to the spot where he would throw off the saddle, winked appreciatively at the watching group before he went after them.

"Ain't that a peach of a horse?" he called back over his shoulder, and with one accord the men of the Lady Slipper agreed with him.

Three H, always cumbersome in his movements when there was no need for haste, got up from under the wagon from where he had been sprawling, stretched his great, muscle-knotted arms high above his head, gave a prodigious yawn, and slouched over to where Hawkins was loosening the latigo. Hawkins, glancing up when he heard the footsteps, looked across the back of his horse and every nerve in him seemed to go taut on the instant, although he merely said—"Hello"—in that impersonal tone with which we address strangers.

Three H went closer with that steady heaviness of movement that marked him at times, and laid a hand upon the horse's shoulder.

"Hello . . . stranger," he said in his gruff way. "I didn't ketch your name."

"Hawkins," said the other, with a perceptible emphasis, his eyes fixed unswervingly upon the face of Three H.

"Holt's mine. They call me Three H here. Good horse yuh got."

"He ain't so bad." Hawkins threw down the saddle and

stepped forward to remove the bridle. His attitude did not
invite further conversation, and Three H backed, swayed his
body in harmony with his mental hesitation, stood for a
moment regarding the other from under his shaggy eyebrows,
and spoke heavily: "You didn't bring no bedroll. You can
crawl between my blankets if yuh want to. I got lots uh
room." With that he turned and went to the tent without so
much as a backward glance to see if Hawkins were going to
reply.

Owlie, standing near them, laughed. "That's more words
than Three H has used in the whole time he's been here," he
observed companionably to the newcomer. "Wonder what
struck him?"

"Who's the little fellow?" Brant Whipple inquired, grinning after the big slouching figure.

"You know as much as anybody," Owlie answered him
in the tone of one who would like to gossip and who is
inclined to resent the lack of material. "His name is Holt . . .
H. H. Holt, he *says.* Claims to come from down south somewhere. We call him Three H. He don't talk none, and he
looks like he'd eat 'em alive, and some uh the boys kinda walk
around him. Hawkins, here, is the first man that seems to
look good to him."

Hawkins smoothed down the mane of his horse with his
hand, pulled the forelock solicitously straight and away from
the animal's eyes, gave him a parting slap on the silky-coated
rump, and sent him off to join the saddle bunch grazing upon
a nearby hillside. Hawkins did not say anything and he did
not look as if the subject interested him. When Bird had
trotted away, however, he made himself a cigarette and spoke
one sentence that might apply to Three H.

"Lots of men have scraped acquaintance with me because
they admire Bird," Hawkins said simply, and walked away to

smoke his cigarette down by the creek and watch the fish
jump for flies in the still places. Brant would have gone with
him, but certain misdeeds of Brant's might or might not be
overlooked by the boss of the Lady Slipper; Brant felt that he
ought to give Lockie a chance to fire him if he were so
minded. He went back to the cook tent and Owlie followed,
curious to hear what Lockie had to say.

Lockie said nothing at all. When it was plain that he did
not mean to remember anything irregular in Brant's past, the
men of the Lady Slipper discussed lazily the stranger
standing, straight and slim, fifty yards away, absorbed in his
own thoughts and in watching the fish. They questioned
Brant, but he knew very little and said so. He had met
Hawkins in the hospital where Hawkins was being treated for
a carbuncle on the back of his neck. Their beds had stood
close together in the convalescent ward, and, being
cowpunchers in distress with the fraternity of their calling,
they had "throwed in together," as Brant put it.

"And you bet he's an all right boy," Brant finished his brief
explanation. "Kinda quiet and thinks a lot of that horse, Bird.
I'm willing to bet he can deliver the goods on them bad actors
in the rough string."

If Brant had wagered anything, he would have won. In the
next week Hawkins proved beyond a doubt that he could
"deliver the goods". Also, he was quiet as Brant had said, and
he certainly showed plenty of affection for his horse, for all
horses in fact, as the Lady Slipper was speedily to have dem-
onstrated to them.

The roundup crew had moved to one of their line camps
and were using the corrals there for their work, as is the way
of men who take whatever good may come to hand. In a small
corral that held the saddle bunch, Owlie was sweating and

swearing, and the little gray he had just roped was sitting back stubbornly with his neck stretched taut and his eyes rolling in anger, trying to express his objection to being led anywhere. Other men were catching their horses and saddling them, and paid no attention to the troubles of Owlie, who was in the habit of fighting his mounts. When, however, the gray gave an unexpected lunge and nearly knocked Owlie down, young Bill thought it wise to lead his own horse hastily outside. "There'll sure be something doing now," he predicted, peering through the rails.

For perhaps five minutes, however, there was nothing to cause comment. Owlie, purple with the mood he was in, got the horse saddled and led him outside the gate, tied him to a post, and went searching silently for something. Presently he picked up a stout club and turned malignantly to the gray. Then began one of those scenes that proclaim men mere brutes. More than one man eyed Owlie dubiously, disgust and disapproval showing plainly in their faces but with the memory of their own lapses from gentleness holding them back from interference.

Bill led his own horse around the corral where he would not be compelled to watch the beating, and remarked that somebody ought to take a club to Owlie and learn *him* something.

Just then Hawkins came running up, his face white with anger. He did not say a word. He rushed at Owlie, grabbed the uplifted club with one hand, and with the other knocked him sprawling in the dust. When Owlie had crawled away from the plunging gray and got up, Hawkins went at him again.

To round out the incident properly, Owlie should have received a thrashing that he would remember—but incidents do not always end properly. Owlie was a fighting man—and

Hawkins got the worst of it. Bill and Brant Whipple at last pulled Owlie off, and Hawkins staggered to his feet and stood leaning against the corral while he stanched the blood streaming from his nose.

"All right," he said. He pulled himself together and looked around at the circle of faces, coming back to Owlie with a glance that had in it plenty of meaning—although one eye was fast closing. "All right . . . you licked me. I'll remember that, and the next time you go beating up a horse, I'll buy into the game with a six-gun. I've watched how you act up with horses, and, if you don't quit it, I'll kill you!"

With that he went off to the cook tent to beg a slice of raw beef for his black eye, but he watched over his shoulder until he saw that Owlie was saddling the gray as peaceably as possible, and that he rode away without even indulging his ill feeling by means of his spurs.

The effect of the fight upon the Lady Slipper outfit was not startling, but it was noticeable to one gifted with the power of observation. When Hawkins was near, men with hasty tempers appeared to be cultivating the virtue of patience and refrained from kicking their horses in the ribs when they were saddling, or "working them over" with clubs. Not even to Brant Whipple did Hawkins ever mention the subject. While he might have been excused for holding a grudge against Owlie, he seemed disposed to overlook the incident—only he was not permitted to do so, because Owlie would not speak to him and was guilty of sneering as openly as he dared.

Bird had speedily become the most popular horse in the outfit, and that not so much because of his beauty as for his unfearing friendliness. When it pleased him to do so, he fed decorously with the saddle bunch; when, however, the fancy seized him or he heard the voice of Hawkins in camp, he walked up to the tents, invited caresses from the men, and teased the cook for biscuits and sugar.

No normal man may withstand the blandishments of such a horse. Even Lockie, the self-restrained, was seen more than once with his arm flung over Bird's neck while he rubbed the soft, silky nose and spoke foolishly in his ears, and he was known to carry sugar in his pockets. Brant Whipple shamelessly taught Bird to smoke cigarettes, and even the stolid Three H frequently lumbered up and gravely shook hands with the horse—and at all these things Owlie curled his lip.

Such then was the standing of Hawkins and Bird with the Lady Slipper when the roundup, with a herd of cows and calves for the weaning, swung back toward the home ranch.

Hawkins and Brant Whipple, riding in together to camp one day, saw a horseman dip suddenly into a shallow gully, slide immediately up into view again, and come thundering toward them, and, without knowing why, they spurred to meet him.

"It's Three H," Brant observed unnecessarily, and then they pulled up facing him.

The eyes of Three H glowed under his shaggy eyebrows, and he breathed like a man who has been running. "Git on this fresh horse uh mine and pull out!" he blurted, staring at Hawkins, and dismounted hurriedly.

Hawkins's mouth straightened a bit, but he made no move to obey. "Why?" he demanded sharply.

Three H stared up at him, and his body swayed awkwardly as it was wont to do when his brain was working. "Why . . . they're after you . . . and Silvertip. Stock inspector's in camp, waiting for yuh to ride in. I got your slicker and some grub with me. They was looking at Silvertip and didn't see me. Maybe you can git an hour's start, if yuh hurry." He hooked a stirrup over the horn and began fumbling the knot of his latigo with fingers made awkward by his anxiety.

"You needn't unsaddle," Hawkins told him coolly. "Now how do yuh reckon they located me up here?" He folded his hands over his saddle horn and stared hard at the prairie sod beneath him. "It's been two years and over," he went on meditatively. "I made sure I was dead safe."

"What's it all about?" Brant peered into Hawkins's bloodless face and spoke for the first time.

Hawkins lifted his head and looked at him for a moment. "Horse stealing," he snapped out. "I haven't any license to keep Bird . . . or Silvertip, as Holt calls him."

Brant winced, for horse stealing is an ugly word among men. "Well, you better pile on Three H's horse and drift," he advised after the shock of the bald statement was over. "The jasper that's holding down the stock inspector job in this county is a sure-enough snake when he's after a man."

Hawkins had gone back to studying the ground, but he looked up again. "I'm thinking of Bird," he said simply.

Three H gazed at him, open-mouthed. "They've got him in camp . . . tied up to the bed wagon," he said stolidly, and added uneasily: "We ain't got much time."

Hawkins turned his eyes to the west where the sky was reddening with the sunset. "And they'll take him back, and hand him over to Jim Bradley. And Jim will leave him stand tied up in front of some building all night in the cold and rain, and spur him all the way home and beat him over the head when he gets him there, and then let Bird stand in the corral without feed or water till Jim gets ready to tend him."

He turned savagely to Three H, but he still spoke with calm bitterness. "You know how it was, Holt. You know how it'll be again. You know I'd've bought Bird if Jim would've sold him . . . but he wouldn't. You. . . ." His eyes narrowed with a sudden suspicion. "Was it you put 'em next?"

Swaying like a huge dancing bear, Three H left his horse and came toward the two. "I ain't that kind," he protested gruffly. "I don't sleep in the same blankets with a man and then give him the double-cross. I want you to git away. I brought you some grub and your slicker and a fresh horse. I don't know how they found out . . . but yuh better not stand here talking about it. Yuh better go."

Hawkins smiled queerly. "Yes," he agreed, his suspicion of Three H leaving him as quickly as it had come. "I reckon I better, all right." He pricked his horse gently with the spurs and started off at a sharp canter. "Much obliged!" he called back as an afterthought, "for putting me wise!"

Three H bellowed after him: "Hold on . . . yuh ain't got the grub!"

"Give it to me!" cried Brant, reaching down for it. "He acts like he was plumb rattled!" With the little bundle tied up in a dirty flour sack swaying in his hand, he spurred after Hawkins and presently overtook him. "Here, you'll need this!" he called out, looking curiously at the other, for Hawkins did not look rattled. Instead, from the grim set of his face, he was a man filled with the determination to do one thing and do it successfully, without faltering and without failure. Only—and Brant's eyebrows were pulled together in a puzzled frown because of it—Hawkins was headed straight for camp.

He took the little bundle of food and crowded it into his coat pocket while he galloped. "Thanks," he said absently. Then he added: "Your gun's the same as mine. Yuh got any spare shells you can let me have?"

Wolves were numerous and bold that fall, and Brant had his gun buckled on. He pushed a dozen cartridges from the little loops in his belt and gave them to Hawkins. "You ain't thinking of killing off the stock inspector and getting away with Bird, are yuh?" he questioned disapprovingly. "Because I can tell yuh right now, Lockie won't stand for no such play. Lockie's so law-abiding he'd turn out the whole outfit to run yuh down."

"Thanks!" said Hawkins dryly, shoving the cartridges into the empty spaces on his own belt. "It's handy to know all these things."

Brant twitched his shoulders impatiently, for he could not tell from the tone whether Hawkins spoke in earnest or whether he meant to be sarcastic. "Well, you're acting like a chump, anyway," he said.

Three H, delayed because he had to recinch his saddle, galloped up behind them, and his gorilla face was comical in its perturbation. "Where yuh going?" he called out hoarsely to Hawkins. "Yuh don't need to give yourself up . . . I'll help yuh out all I kin. You been leery of me ever since yuh found me here, but yuh needn't to be. I know yuh for a white man." Which was a good deal for Three H to say, as was evident from the manner in which he blundered through the speech.

"Thanks," said Hawkins for the third time. After a moment he turned his face squarely toward them so that they caught the somber glow in his eyes. "You boys got any smoking you can let me have . . . and matches?" he asked. Then, meeting briefly the troubled gaze of Three H, he added quietly: "I'm not aiming to walk up and hold out my hands for the irons."

"Well, what in thunder . . . ?" began Brant, hastily emptying his pockets of tobacco, papers, and matches, and finally failing to finish the sentence because he realized the utter uselessness of questioning the man. Plainly he meant to escape if possible, else he would not have begged the cartridges and the smoking material. Studying the matter while they rode leisurely through the afterglow to camp—leisurely because

Hawkins was setting the pace and seemed to wish it—Brant decided that Hawkins meant to take Bird with him. A crazy notion it was, with not one chance in a hundred that he would succeed, but it gave a thrill to Brant's blood for its very daring.

"You can't get Bird outta camp," Three H stated bluntly. "He's tied up to the bed wagon and. . . ."

Hawkins turned irritably toward him. "I wish you fellows would quit beefing around about it," he snapped. "*I* know what I'm going to do . . . and nothing could stop me!"

Naturally that ended all speech upon the subject. Hawkins rode with his eyes fixed straight, glancing neither to the right nor the left, guiding his horse mechanically around the half-sunken boulders that dotted sparely the bald upland. Brant, stealing sidelong glances toward him, saw his teeth go hard together once, but the *click* of them was lost in the saddle sounds and the beat of the horses' hoofs upon the gravelly soil. What passed in his friend's mind, Brant would have given much to read. The thoughts were bitter ones, such as some men never know in all their lives.

They dipped down into a long, winding coulée that led to the river, and the night shadows came sweeping up to meet them. Hawkins looked down into the coulée's bottom, twitched the reins, and, obedient to the signal, his horse hurried his pace and went sliding down the deep-worn cow trail at a shuffling trot.

Dark little gullies, rock-rimmed and strewn thickly with boulders, wound crazily back into the hills the riders were leaving behind. Few of the gullies offered even a precarious passage for horsemen, and it occurred to Brant that a man could easily hide himself away from pursuit and even escape altogether if he were wary and not visited by misfortune.

It would seem as if Hawkins himself were weighing the

chances, for he glanced sharply into the gullies as he galloped past, and once or twice he turned in the saddle to look again.

They neared the mouth of the main coulée, rode out upon the river bottom near camp, and Hawkins pulled up suddenly. After that he went slowly, and the others guessed that he wished to approach camp as quietly as possible. They wondered why, but, like good friends, they yielded to his unexpressed desire without understanding his design; for that reason their arrival, while expected, was not observed.

"You . . . chump," muttered Brant uselessly when Hawkins, the length of his horse in the lead, rode boldly up within ten paces of the group near the bed wagon.

Bird, scenting his master, lifted his head, perked his ears forward, and nickered softly, but for the first time he got no answer.

"Well, I'm here," Hawkins announced cheerfully, singling out the one strange figure which started forward from the group. "Heard yuh wanted to see me. That right?"

"I guess it is," retorted the stranger in a tone of finality. "And I guess you know why. I'll have to ask you for your gun."

Hawkins was staring through the dusk at Bird, treading with dainty impatience where he stood chafing at the unaccustomed confinement of the short rope, and he did not seem to hear. Bird nickered again coaxingly, and Hawkins swallowed hard.

"I said I want your gun . . . and get off your horse," repeated the inspector.

"Oh . . . sure!" Hawkins reached to his hip, fired with the next movement of his arm—and the shot went true. He wheeled and went galloping into the gloom with the roar of the inspector's gun close behind him, the bullets whining by his ears.

"Get after him, you fellows!" shouted the inspector while he ran to his own horse, furious at being caught so easily.

But Brant and Three H urged their horses up to the pitiful heap beside the bed wagon—the heap that had been Bird.

"That's why he come to camp," Three H said stolidly. "He didn't want Bird to go back to Jim Bradley and git abused like he used to be. That's why he stole him . . . 'cause Jim abused him."

The men of the Lady Slipper surged up, looked down at the quivering, coppery-red body, and then understandingly at one another. Hawkins—none but Hawkins would dare so much for the sake of a horse. From afar came the clatter of the inspector's horse galloping over the loose rocks that strewed the coulée mouth. They heard him shout angrily back at the camp before he disappeared.

Then Lockie came back mentally to present urgencies. "Get your horses and get out there and take a hand!" he commanded harshly. "When an officer calls on yuh for help, you better move!" Then he added one sentence, which proved him a big-hearted range rider first and a foreman afterward—and which also turned the tide in favor of Hawkins and made his escape not only possible, but probable.

"Make a showing, anyhow!" was what he told them, and the men of the Lady Slipper understood.

The Infernal Feminine

Bower had attended plenty of area dances, and knew the people and customs well. She must have had great fun writing this *tour-de-force* that exposed classic male-female conflicts and prejudices with a brilliant rôle switch. "The Infernal Feminine" was published in the March, 1907 issue of *The Popular Magazine*. The Happy Family of the Flying U teases diminutive, cherubic, touchy Pink Perkins about being in love. He responds with a threat involving the outfit's guest, a *second* lady doctor (another rarity in Western fiction). An unusual bet evolves. The entire outfit then chooses costumes for the Thanksgiving dance. Pink enlists the aid of the imaginative home ranch ladies in creating the ultimate whizzer for a truly diabolic revenge.

"Where's Pink at?" It was Cal, coming into the bunkhouse late, who put the question to the Happy Family as a whole.

"Where's he's always at lately . . . and that's up at the White House getting his fingers doctored." Jack Bates rolled over upon his side and reached for his cigarette book. "Them fingers uh his takes more fixing than a broken leg. For half a dollar I'd burn *my* fingers with a rope, and get into the game. And *he's* the lad that's got no use for girls!"

"Doctor Cecil's all right, you bet. Yuh can't blame Pink for needing treatment bad . . . especially when he's got a bunch uh gratitude coming for rescuing her from that old cow. I'd absorb all the gratitude she was of a mind to hand out, myself. But a fellow with a rep like Pink's got. . . ."

"Cadwolloper's in love," stated Weary calmly.

Pink, opening the door at that instant, heard the remark and came in upon them stormily. His hand was freshly and scientifically bandaged in clean, white linen, and his yellow curls were brushed into shiny rings, and his gray hat perched upon them at a jaunty angle.

"I'd like to know where yuh got the papers for saying that?" he cried belligerently to Weary. "When I'm in love, I'll let yuh know."

"Love"—Weary smiled placidly—"speaks right up for itself. Yuh don't need to tell us, Cadwolloper . . . we aren't impolite enough to ask for embarrassing details. Yuh got all the symptoms, and that's all we need to go by."

"Symptoms uh what?" Pink glared around at them. "Can't a man get his hand done up without being woozy over the girl that does it? Yuh don't know a darn' thing about it. Yuh just set down here and chin like a bunch uh darn old granny-gossips. If yuh just had some knittin'-work and check aprons on, you'd be complete. And who do yuh think I'm in love with, since you're so blame wise? The Countess?"

"By golly, no!" blurted Slim jealously. "Mis' Bixby ain't wastin' no time on yeller-haired kids . . . she'd *spank* yuh if yuh went foolin' around *her*."

Weary looked at the others and shook his head commiseratingly.

"Cadwolloper's sure got the symptoms," he said sadly. "It's only a matter uh time, now. Yuh know how it worked on Chip . . . had the Little Doctor pull him through with a twisted ankle, and . . . it was all off with the big cowpuncher. A rope burn ain't quite so serious, but, mama! It'll do the business, all right . . . especially when a man's done the heroic act *getting* them slight disablements. When he's saved the girl from an angry bossy cow, and burnt his fingers doing it, why, it's quite sufficient. How's the fingers coming on, Cadwolloper? They're sure getting good care."

"None uh your damn' business!" snapped Pink.

"It always does make 'im irritable," mused Weary. "Yuh remember Chip was right on the fight, when the malady first commenced working in his blood. Yuh couldn't point your finger toward him without getting cussed. It's like measles. . . ." Weary dodged in time, and looked at Pink reproachfully. "I'm sure surprised at yuh, Cadwolloper. It's getting plumb serious, when yuh turn on your friends that way."

"What the whole bunch uh yuh needs," Pink retorted loftily, "is to pace along up to the house and get your *heads* poulticed. The sooner some uh your curious ideas are drawed out, the healthier it'll be for yuh. Well, darn yuh!" Pink turned truculently upon Irish Mallory, who was a newcomer and Weary's cousin and second self—so far as looks went. "What's eating you? Yuh sound like a jug uh whisky when Slim's applied to the little end."

"Nothing . . . but it sure amuses me to watch a man that's got his."

"Watch out, or you'll get yours, and get it sudden!" threatened Pink sullenly.

The Family laughed. Pink stood just five feet, five inches in his riding boots, and Irish towered over him to a slim, muscular height of six feet, two inches—also in his riding boots. He could have carried Pink about in his arms like a baby, and he had a fighting reputation almost equal to Pink's.

"Oh, you fellows make me plumb sick!" Pink cried above the laughter.

"Better go up and get Doctor Cecil to give yuh something for it, by golly!" advised Slim solemnly.

That from Slim went beyond Pink's endurance. A white streak began to show plainly around his mouth and nostrils, and his eyes were so deep a purple that they looked quite black in the lamplight. He could not fight the whole Family, much as he would like to do so, but he could hint darkly at vengeance.

"This'll be about enough on the subject uh love," he said in his clear treble. "Every darn' one uh you has had your dose of it . . . and you'll likely get another. Cal's got a girl he's plumb batty over, and Weary's schoolma'am is about the only thing that ever happened. Happy Jack's got it virulent, and Slim's like a sick yearling when the Countess is around. Jack Bates is taking absent-treatment for his, and Irish . . . well, if Irish ain't had an attack lately, he likely will. I hope I may be there to see it, for he'll sure have it bad. So far as I'm concerned, I've been vaccinated, and it worked fine. I ain't got the ailment, and there ain't any use in you fellows getting excited over it . . . there's nothing to it, I tell yuh. But it don't drop here. You've said a lot, and, before I'm through with yuh, you'll swallow every darn' word, and here's hoping they don't set easy in your digestive apparatus. It's all right now . . . but, mind what I tell you, you've sure got it coming!"

Someone started the applause, and the others took it up derisively. Irish uncoiled himself and passed his hat around solemnly, and took up an assorted collection of burnt matches, cigarette stubs, and the like, and presented it gravely to Pink. Pink accepted the offering without a word, deposited it in an empty tobacco sack, and grinned.

"All right . . . I'll take this up to Doctor Cecil, so she can hand it back to you . . . sometime."

"Aw, go on!" Irish looked a bit startled. "Don't be a fool."

"So help me, Josephine, this goes to Doctor Cecil . . . and, when you get yours, she'll return the offering! Oh, I'll fix you aplenty!" Pink turned and darted out before they could stop him, and, when they craned necks out of the door, they saw him heading straight up the hill to the white house.

"He won't dare," Irish tried to assure himself by saying.

"Yes, he will . . . the little devil," said Jack Bates gloomily. "He'll tell her every word we said."

"On second thought," Weary remarked meditatively, breaking a match-stub in his fingers and casting the pieces far from him, "I take it all back. Cadwolloper ain't in love."

The second coming of Doctor Cecil Granthum to the ranch had been the precursor of some agitation in the Happy Family. Some of them rather resented her coming, as likely to break into their accustomed life of happy-go-lucky unconventionality. The Little Doctor they were used to, and looked upon her quite as one of themselves—especially since Dell had become Mrs. Chip Bennett. The Countess was "part of the scenery", as Weary said. Other women might come for a day or two, and no one minded. But Doctor Cecil was out to remain indefinitely, and she was the sort of girl one can't ignore.

She was a head taller than the Little Doctor, and she had a fluffy pompadour that always had stray wisps breaking from their moorings and blowing about. She had big, blue eyes that saw a lot they weren't intended to see, and a way of saying things that made one uncomfortably aware that she knew all one's weaknesses. Those who she had met before—Weary, Cal, and Happy Jack, Slim and Jack Bates—she ordered about and bullied. Pink and Irish Mallory she stood off and studied quite openly.

For these reasons, they stood a bit in awe of Doctor Cecil Granthum, and the bare threat from Pink to tell her what they had been saying was disquieting to the Happy Family. That Pink, after rescuing the energetic young woman from an irate cow, should quite openly show his liking for her was bad enough; that he should openly, traitorously repeat their remarks concerning that liking was worse. The Happy Family took an attitude of guarded defiance, and wondered if Pink would really tell her.

For a week their behavior was circumspect in the extreme and their manner toward Pink nothing short of placating, after which peace hovered over the Flying U bunkhouse, and the Happy Family breathed freer. Pink, evidently, did not hold any grudge against them.

They put heads together amicably and began to discuss costumes for the Thanksgiving masquerade ball in Dry Lake. They were all going, and they intended to add a good bit to the spectacle, and to the excitement as well—for it was rumored that Fort Benton had wakened from her lethargy and was boastfully preparing to send a delegation that could teach Dry Lake things about costumes and fine dancing. Dry Lake, it may be remarked, was not enthusiastic over being taught things by Fort Benton, or any other place. Dry Lake was a self-sufficient little place, and jealous of its dignity.

"I'm going as an Injun squaw," said Happy Jack, with an air of one suddenly inspired. "I betcha nobody'll know *me!*"

"Yuh want to disguise them feet, then," Irish Mallory remarked caustically. "They ain't easy forgot."

"Irish and me had better tog up alike," said Weary hastily to head off any war-like reply from Happy Jack. "We'll sure keep 'em guessing some. What you going to wear, Cadwolloper?"

"I'm going as a chink. I've got the proper build, and, when yuh see me hully-hully chop-chopee through the crowd, yuh can't tell it from the real thing."

"Well, you fellows can tip your hands if yuh want to," said Jack Bates, "but me, I don't tell what I'm aiming to look like."

"Chip says the Little Doctor's got a catalogue uh costumes up to the house, and we can club together and rent anything we like. Run up and borrow it, Pink. This thing has got to be put through right." Cal stared around at them with big, earnest, blue eyes.

"Well, but I bid for the chink . . . yuh don't want to forget that," warned Pink, and departed on the errand.

When he returned, they hunched closely together, and light hair mingled with brown while they debated earnestly the merits of pictured costumes.

Pink clung steadfastly to the idea of being a Chinaman, selected the rig, and marked it with a very black cross.

Happy Jack wavered uncertainly between an "Injun squaw" and Satan—until Weary and Irish settled the matter by announcing that they would both be devils, whereupon Happy sighed and marked the squaw for himself.

It was late that night when they slept, and then a few of them dreamed strange things. The next night they went again critically over the catalogue, confirmed their choices, and went up in a body to ask the Little Doctor to send for the things and to make sure she did not mix the order. They measured one another solemnly with the Little Doctor's tape, and swore her to secrecy, although that was superfluous; they knew they could trust Mrs. Chip.

Then they waited impatiently and talked of little else. The costumes came, and they were up till three o'clock in the morning, trying them on and practicing fancy steps and guying one another as only the Happy Family can do.

Weary was proud of his rig—a blue devil, it was, and appropriate because of its contrast with his disposition. Irish was a yellow devil, and Pink made the most adorable Chinaman one could imagine. Happy Jack perspired over his squaw costume, and Jack Bates tucked a mysterious bundle under his pillow; he was still resolutely refraining from "tipping his hand", and the Happy Family, beyond teasing him a bit, let him alone, too much interested in their own affairs to be over-curious. Slim's rig was blatantly Dutch.

So it was for two nights, and then came disaster to Pink. In the night they heard him swearing softly between groans, and in the morning found him with a rampant toothache, which not even the skill of the two doctors up at the house could dispel. The bunkhouse reeked with the odor of drugs, and Pink's temper was something to avoid rousing.

"Yuh got to git it stopped before tomorrow night," reminded Happy Jack dolefully, "or there'll be one chink missing at the dance."

"Oh, shut up!" growled Pink, his voice muffled in his pillow.

The reek of drugs grew more pronounced as Pink's efforts to stop the pain redoubled. The Happy Family advised having the Little Doctor pull the offending tooth, and Pink swore at them for answer.

On the morning of the dance, his cheek was swollen perceptibly under the silk neckerchief he used for a bandage, and Happy Jack croaked commiseratingly. It was all off, he reminded Pink often; he could not go to the dance, and he was out just five dollars, for he'd have to pay for the Chinese costume just the same.

Pink threw things at Happy Jack, and nursed his face in his hands, and was not cheerful company. The Happy Family was sympathetic, and Weary even offered to stay at home to keep him company. Pink remarked that the tooth was all the company he wanted, and that he'd be darned glad when they were gone, so he could be let alone. As for the dance, he would be glad when it was over so they'd quit yapping about it; he was sick of hearing about blue devils and squaw togs, and seeing Jack Bates feel under his pillow every two minutes.

He wished they'd pull out and leave him alone. As for the Chinese clothes, he told Happy Jack, caustically, that he needn't worry over that five dollars—it didn't come out of *his* wages.

So they wrapped their costumes carefully and departed for Dry Lake, and left Pink to the questionable comfort of an empty bunkhouse and a cheek twice its natural size. They were very sorry, but there was nothing that they could do for him, so they put his woes rapidly behind them and, when they reached Dry Lake and the atmosphere of mystery and preparation, forgot him utterly.

Irish Mallory, standing beside Weary near the door, ran his eyes appraisingly along the benches that lined the wall. Not having a girl of his own, he was free, and anxious to choose the best. He glanced the second time at a tall, dignified college girl who he guessed to be Doctor Cecil Granthum, and at the Little Doctor in a star-spangled domino beside her.

He would like very much to dance with Doctor Cecil, but she always seemed to be studying him impersonally as a new species of trouble germ, or something—he did not quite know what. He sighed and looked further.

Ten feet beyond, a lithe, gay-clad figure stood fingering a gaudily beribboned tambourine and tapping the floor impatiently with the toe of one high-heeled red slipper. Irish had once upon a time heard "Carmen" sung, and he recognized intuitively that this piquant, Gypsyish figure was none other than the mischievous Carmen herself. She turned her head idly, caught his glance upon her, and flirted her tambourine coyly. Irish nudged Weary, and asked who she was.

"Can't read her brand from here," the blue devil answered. "But I take her to be one uh the Benton crowd.

204

Mama, she's sure a peacherine."

The next minute Irish was making his way toward her, the lust of possession in his eyes. They swung off together in a two-step, and Irish felt that luck was with him; the lithe young Carmen not only bewitched the eye, she danced distractingly. He began to feel glad that the Benton crowd had come among them.

Cal Emmett saw them whirl by and stared after them curiously. Jack Bates promised himself the next dance with the Spanish-looking girl with the tambourine jingling when she moved, and with the white arms loaded with quaint bracelets and the spangly things in her long black hair.

They flocked around Irish and his partner in a way to turn a girl's head with vanity, but the girl only laughed at them wickedly and tapped them reprovingly with the tambourine when they crowded too close, and recklessly promised dances to them all. Irish frowned behind his mask, and asked them in a whisper, where were their papers for cutting in, and why didn't they go dance with their partners.

Happy Jack lumbered up and stared at the dazzling center of the circle and was sorry that he had elected to be a squaw. Squaws may scarce hope to win much notice from feminine dancers. Then Slim came by, stopped to see what was going on, and lingered, fascinated by the saucy challenge in the bright eye of Carmen. He quite forgot that he had intended asking the Countess for the next quadrille, and stared dumbly, till Irish almost dragged her away to dance again.

After that, one would think that the Happy Family owned this strange beauty from Benton. Others might crave the pleasure of a dance with her, but they never experienced it. Jack Bates captured her for a waltz, and surrendered her reluctantly to Irish for another two-step. Cal Emmett almost fought for a quadrille, and Slim begged abjectly for any dance she was willing to give him. Even Chip came up and danced a schottische with her, and Weary tried hard enough to get a number, but was always a half second too late.

Word was passed indignantly around among the faithful that the Happy Family had traitorously ignored the tacit boycott and had gone over in a body to the Benton crowd. Dry Lake had meant to snub the Benton faction and leave them to dance with one another or be wallflowers, as they chose. Dry Lake did not approve the imbecile attitude of the Happy Family.

Even the Little Doctor was left for second choice, and Doctor Cecil had only one dance with each—barring Irish, who never went near her. He was frankly and unmistakably infatuated with the girl of the tambourine, and he seemed not to care how many knew it.

Then, between dances, she slipped away into the ladies' dressing room, and from there Irish lost sight of her for a time. The squaw came up and beckoned mysteriously to the yellow devil.

"Say, yuh want t' watch out for that red-and-yeller girl uh your'n," he warned in an undertone. "I seen her slip outdoors, and Bert Rogers says he seen her slip outdoors, and Bert Rogers says he seen her hitting the bottle cached at the corner uh the steps. I knowed she was pretty fly . . . the way she was throwin' goo-goo eyes at me."

"If she made eyes at you," the yellow devil retorted cuttingly, "it shows she ain't fly . . . she's just plain crazy! I guess yuh hit that bottle once too often yourself."

"Aw, gwan!" adjured the squaw, in Happy's well-known tone of general refutation, "I ain't been near it. I knowed all the time that Benton crowd was pretty tough, and, if that red-slipper peach uh yours ain't a sport. . . ."

"That's about all from you," grated Irish in a voice that

made Happy back up precipitately. Irish had not been with the Happy Family long, but, nevertheless, he was known to be unsafe when he spoke like that.

Irish waited near the dressing room door, and, when the girl finally appeared, he claimed her defiantly in the very face of Happy, who hung around to watch. The girl's eyes danced more bewitchingly than before, and, when they stood in the quadrille waiting for the music, she caught the hand of Irish and danced a few steps with an abandon that was irresistible —and shocking. At least Dry Lake was not in tolerant mood where any from Benton was concerned, and masked faces turned toward the daring young Carmen, and then turned haughtily away. Irish felt himself grow hot behind the sinister face of Satan, but he held his head high and pressed the hand of the girl quite openly and shamelessly.

When they saluted their partners, Carmen swept him an elaborate and conspicuous curtsy, and swung off in the dance with her abandon in no wise abated. Irish caught more than once a familiar odor on her breath—an odor that the Un-written Law makes permissible only to the masculine sex. He was worried, but staunch.

The next dance was an Oxford minuet—a dance with pos-sibilities, but which is danced discreetly by the young women of Dry Lake who choose to ignore the possibilities. Carmen, dancing with Cal Emmett, was not discreet; neither did she ignore the possibilities. In the cross-steps, her red slippers went high—oh, very high. To be plain, she kicked. And her tambourine kept rollicky intoxicating time with her toes. Cal Emmett, feeling the eyes of his girl, Len Adams, upon him, perspired guiltily behind his mask. Dry Lake—or all of it that witnessed the performance—went beyond being merely shocked; it was horrified.

Weary and Chip gravitated together as by common consent, and Happy Jack and Slim joined them anxiously. The dance was ended, and the dancers were ranged along the wall with a space between themselves and Carmen. She flirted her tambourine shamelessly and hummed a little tune under her breath.

"We can't stay in such company as *that*," Chip announced in a tone of finality. "You fellows can do as you like . . . but I'm going to take Dell and Cecil home."

"If she keeps up that gait, they'll *all* go," said Weary. "My schoolma'am won't stay, anyhow."

"By golly, neither will the Countess!" said Slim.

"What's the committee thinking about?" Chip demanded. "If it was me, she'd go . . . and go quick."

"Say, I've been trying to square myself with Len Adams," complained Cal, coming up. "She sure turned me down hard. Darn that little rip, she might uh made a show uh herself with somebody else . . . she sure has queered me with Len!"

"Well, let's round up our women and pull out," suggested Chip. "The committee isn't going to do anything about it, from the looks."

They trooped off to find their partners, and not one of them but remembered guiltily their eagerness of an hour before to dance with the brazen young person in the red slippers. They hoped the girls had not noticed.

"You've been dancing with her yourself," the Little Doctor told Chip calmly, when he announced his decision. "You seemed very anxious of the pleasure . . . if she's good enough for all you fellows to dance with, it surely won't hurt us to stay in the same hall with her. *We* haven't sought her acquaintance."

"But she's been drinking," protested Chip, a bit staggered by the attack. "There's no telling what she'll do next. Nobody knew at first but what she was all right. You can't stay with a

. . . a person of that caliber."

"I'm not staying with her," said the Little Doctor tartly. "No, you boys were almost ready to fight each other over dancing with her, not an hour ago . . . she can't be much worse now than she was then. She isn't hurting *us* any . . . and you needn't dance with her unless you want to. Cecil and I are going to *stay*."

To prove it, the Little Doctor went off to waltz with Bert Rogers, and left Chip staring after her indignantly.

The schoolma'am, when she discovered that the Little Doctor would not go, elected also to remain, and Len Adams, not being in a mood to speak to Cal Emmett on any subject, was therefore unapproachable. Slim tried the Countess, but she did not want to go unless Dell went.

The Happy Family gathered in the corner by the water bucket and discussed the situation gloomily, while they watched the offending red slippers flash in and out of the crowd, and called one another's attention to the shameless way she was leaning upon the shoulder of Irish. They did not quite know what to do. The squaw came up when the dance was over and announced something with mournful relish.

"She's gone out ag'in," he said. "I seen her taking a sneak, with a big cloak on, but them red slippers give her away. Let's go and keep cases. I betcha she's got a bottle of her own somewheres."

They filed unostentatiously to the door, opened it, and went out under the stars. At first they could see nothing but shafts of dim light where the window shades failed to fit closely, with black shadows between. They moved cautiously, and no one spoke.

Then over against the coal shed, they caught a glimpse of a tiny glow—the glow of a cigarette—and of a slim figure muffled in a dark cloak.

"It's her, all right," whispered Jack Bates. "She's smoking. Now, what do yuh think uh that for a dance supposed to be respectable? If she didn't come straight from a Benton dive."

The figure caught sight of them, evidently. The cigarette was thrown hurriedly away, and she fled swiftly back to the hall. As she ran, she flung back a shrill, derisive epithet—"Rubber, Rubberneck!"—over her shoulder. The Happy Family, stung by the insult, gave chase, although they had not the slightest idea of catching her.

"By golly," said Slim, when they reached the door, "I'm glad Pink ain't here! We'd never hear the last of it."

"Aw, yuh needn't worry . . . he'll hear about it, all right. I betcha somebody'll tell him," mourned Happy, adjusting his mask before he went in, and pulling the black braids of his wig carefully over his shoulders. Happy imagined that he looked a veritable Pocahontas in the rig and was correspondingly fastidious.

"Mama, we sure did act kinda mellow over her, along at first," sighed Weary penitently. "It's 'most too good to keep, and I'm liable to tell Cadwolloper myself. It'll kinda make up to him for missing the show."

"Well, I'm going to have a talk with that fool of a floor manager," declared Chip. "Seeing our women won't go . . . she's got to. This isn't any dance-hall affair, and her absence will be appreciated a lot."

"Yeah, that's what," assented Cal moodily. He was thinking of the figure he had cut in the Oxford minuet, and of Len Adams.

"By golly, when I swung her last time in a quadrille, she hugged me, by golly!" confessed Slim, with his hand on the knob. From within came the shuffle of dancing feet and the *twang* of a guitar, the *tinkle* of a mandolin, and the *wail* of a violin. And above all came the *jangle* of a tambourine as the cause of their worry danced down to that end of the hall.

They went in, and Chip, an austere monk in black domino belted loosely around his middle with a huge silken cord, headed determinedly for the floor manager.

But the floor manager happened to be Jake Dowty, and Jake Dowty happened to have a strong dislike for any and all members of the Happy Family. Also, he had a large idea of his own importance as floor manager.

He received Chip's complaint with chilling neutrality. It was a public dance, he said, and a masquerade at that. He wasn't expected to know who everybody was, or whether they walked in good sassiety. As for him, he hadn't seen anything wrong going on. If Chip—in effect, if not in so many words—didn't like the company he was in, why, there were no strings on him; he could leave.

Chip marched back and reported the conversation almost *verbatim,* and there was indignation in the region of the water bucket. The Happy Family knew less than before just what to do about it.

Dry Lake, they believed, would side with them and against the erring and impenitent Carmen. Still, they were not running the dance, and they had no authority to interfere and say who should participate and who should not.

The only rational thing was, as Dowty had said, to leave if they did not like the company they were in. But they could scarcely leave without the ladies, and the ladies evidently intended to remain.

Chip thought of going again to reason with his Little Doctor, but, knowing his Little Doctor as he did, he realized the futility of further persuasion. She had told him she was going to stay—and it required no effort to imagine that she would do so. And so long as she stayed, it was useless to ask the others to go. They were all—the Little Doctor, the schoolma'am, Len Adams, the Countess, and Doctor Cecil—dancing, and they all appeared to be enjoying themselves very much.

While the Happy Family stood and debated, the girl with the tambourine whirled up in the arms of Irish—Irish still loyal to his first infatuation and still very defiant of the Happy Family's opinion. Carmen swung her tambourine impudently in the very face of Chip as she passed, and brought it down none too lightly upon the brown, indignant head of Weary.

"Rubbernecks!" she jeered insolently as she passed.

But Weary was roused at last, and Weary, once roused, was not to be passed by without notice. He reached a long arm, and caught Irish by the elbow, and spun the two back facing the Happy Family. From sheer surprise they stopped, and other dancers whirled giddily past. Weary kept his hold on the arm of Irish, and Irish, his eyes gleaming warningly through his mask, stood quietly and waited.

"Rubbernecks aren't the worst kind of people in the world," drawled Weary. "Girls that forget to be what the Lord meant them to be is a heap worse, if yuh ask me. And when that kind of a female strays in where she isn't expected or wanted, the best thing she can do is to stray out again . . . and she can't go too soon. I don't believe yuh want to unmask before the crowd, miss, and it's getting close to midnight. It's a beautiful night outside."

The girl shook back her black, jewel-spangled hair and, lifting her tambourine, jingled it under the irate nose of Weary. "Don't you love me any more? Can't you think of any of the nice things you said when we danced together? I dance like thistledown, you know, and you could go on forever. *Is* it a nice night outside? Come, then . . . we'll go and see." She caught Weary by the arm, and pulled gently.

"It strikes me you've been out once too often," he said, standing firm. His voice was a bit sad and reproachful. Weary had all a cowpuncher's reverence for a good woman, and to see one here among the others who was not good struck him as pitiful.

"You just now told me to go," she reminded, still clinging.

"Look here," interposed Irish, husky with anger at them all. "She's in the right. A while back yuh was crazy to be nice to her. Yuh danced with her every chance yuh got, and felt sore because yuh couldn't dance oftener. And I tell yuh right now, she's going to stay if she wants to, and you fellows'll treat her as a lady should be treated, or by thunder you'll answer to me for every insult yuh give her. Come, little girl, we'll get out uh this righteous bunch."

"*Masks off!*" shouted the caller. "Midnight. Everyone unmask where you stand!"

The Happy Family gave no heed to the command. They were waiting to gather breath for the next move in the peculiar struggle in which they found themselves.

"Did you hear? Masks off. I want to see my friends." There was scornful emphasis upon the last word as the girl, with a saucy tinkle of her beribboned tambourine, reached up a white arm and deftly removed the mask she wore.

The Happy Family gasped and went back against the wall.

"Pink . . . you little devil!" It was Cal Emmett, and his eyes were bulging.

"Mama mine! It's Cadwolloper!" Weary gulped, and grabbed Pink affectionately by the shoulder. "Say, how about that tooth?"

"Gum properly applied makes a dandy swelling in the jaw." Pink grinned, jingling the tambourine. "You're a hot bunch, ain't yuh? Think uh the sickening goo-goo slush you've been pouring into my ears all evening! Ain't yuh ashamed uh yourselves? I guess we're about even now!"

"Mister Mallory, I believe this belongs to you," said a calm, clear voice at the elbow of Irish.

Irish turned, stupefied, and received into his outstretched palm a small tobacco-sack half filled with a varied assortment of burnt matches and cigarette stubs.

The Happy Family stared after the straight, retreating form of Doctor Cecil, and gulped their chagrin.

"Cadwolloper, yuh little devil, yuh told her!"

"Sure!"

Pink turned to Irish, still staring down at the token in his hand. "Come on . . . take your girl away from this righteous bunch," he pleaded in the voice of Carmen.

Irish looked down at him, and swore softly through clenched teeth.

About the Author

Bertha Muzzy Bower, born in Cleveland, Minnesota, was the first woman to make a career of writing Western fiction and remains one of the most widely known. She became familiar with cowboys and ranch life at eighteen when her family moved to Great Falls, Montana in 1889. She was nearly thirty and a mother of three before she began writing. Her first novel, CHIP OF THE FLYING U, was initially published as a magazine story in 1904, and was an immediate success. Bower went on to write thirteen more books about the Flying U. In 1933 she turned to stories set prior to the events described in CHIP OF THE FLYING U. THE WHOOP-UP TRAIL begins a trilogy recounting Chip Bennett's arrival in Montana and early adventures at the Flying U. Much of the appeal of Flying U saga is due to Bower's use of humor, the strong sense of loyalty and family depicted among her characters, as well as the authentic quality of her cowboys. She herself was a maverick who experimented with the Western story, introducing modern technologies and raising unusual social concerns—such as aeroplanes in SKYRIDER or divorce in LONESOME LAND. She was sensitive to the lives of women on the frontier and created some extraordinary female characters, notably in Vada Williams in THE HAUNTED HILLS, Georgie Howard in GOOD INDIAN, Helen in THE BELLEHELEN MINE, and Mary Allison in TROUBLE RIDES THE WIND, another early Chip Bennett story. Her work was also memorable for characterization, setting, and dramatization of nature, as in VAN PATTEN or THE SWALLOWFORK BULLS. Her next Five Star Western will be LAW OF THE FLYING U.

About the Editor

Kate Baird Anderson is an artist, writer and voracious reader with many interests, from history, etymology and archeology to needlework, gardening, and the black hole of genealogy. She is currently working on B. M. Bower's biography and Western novel reprints, and editing Bower's short stories, as well as those of grandfather Bertrand W. Sinclair, a noted Canadian author in the 1920s. Kate was born in Los Angeles County in 1929, spent much of her childhood with grandmother Bower, and has also lived in Oregon, Montana, Oklahoma, Arkansas, Indiana, and Northern Illinois.